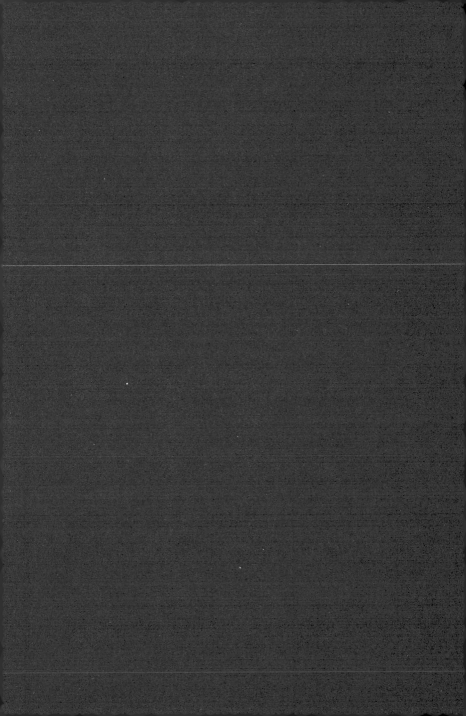

a MIKE & RIEL MYSTERY

HIT AND RUN

NORAH MCCLINTOCK

darbycreek
MINNEAPOLIS

First U.S. edition published in 2014 by Lerner Publishing Group, Inc.

Published by arrangement with Scholastic Canada Ltd.

Darby Creek
A division of Lerner Publishing Group, Inc.
241 First Avenue North
Minneapolis, MN 55401 U.S.A.

For reading levels and more information, look up this title at www.lernerbooks.com.

Front cover: © Jan Stromme/Stone/Getty Images.

Main body text set in Janson Text LT Std 11.5/15
Typeface provided by Adobe Systems.

Library of Congress Cataloging-in-Publication Data

McClintock, Norah.
Hit and run / by Norah McClintock.
p. cm. — (Mike & Riel ; #1)
Originally published by Scholastic Canada, 2003.
Summary: Fifteen-year-old Mike McGill has been living with his Uncle Billy since his mother's death. Only ten years older than Mike, Billy loves to party, and doesn't pay much attention when Mike starts getting in trouble. But Mike's history teacher, an ex-cop name Riel, does pay attention. Especially when long-hidden information starts coming to light that makes it seem that the death of Mike's mother might not have been an accident after all.
ISBN 978–1–4677–2605–4 (lib. bdg. : alk. paper)
ISBN 978–1–4677–2612–2 (eBook)
[1. Mystery and detective stories. 2. Teachers—Fiction.] I. Title.
PZ7.M478414184Hi 2014
[Fic]—dc23 2013017548

Manufactured in the United States of America
1 – SB – 12/31/13

PROLOGUE

"Why?" I said the night before it happened. "Why does Billy have to come over?"

"What's wrong with Billy?" my mother said. "You like Billy."

Sure, I liked Billy. I liked him a lot. He let me watch TV as long as I wanted. All I had to do was promise that I'd scoot upstairs as soon as we heard Mom's footsteps on the porch and that I wouldn't tell on him. And he never made me brush my teeth. He never even mentioned teeth. But that wasn't the point.

"I'm nearly twelve," I said. "I can look after myself. Vin's parents don't get a babysitter for him all the time." Vin was my best friend.

"Well, I'm not Vin's parents," my mother said. "And you're barely eleven. Too young to be left home alone. When you are twelve, we'll talk."

"But that's almost a whole year away."

My mother smiled and kissed my cheek. "Then we'll talk in almost a whole year," she said.

The day it happened, Billy picked me up at Mrs. McNab's, where I usually went after school, and took me home to—I hated the word—babysit me. Still, if I had to have a babysitter—which, if you ask me, I really didn't—Billy was probably the best choice. After all, he was my uncle. Up until a couple of years ago, he had lived with us. Even after he moved out, he came around a lot, usually at supper time. Mom never minded. Well, except lately. Lately, things had been a little rough between the two of them. They'd fought big-time when Billy showed up a while back with an Xbox console for me—an early Christmas present, Billy had called it.

"It's months until Christmas," Mom had said. Then Mom and I had fought when she made Billy take it back.

The day it happened, Mom didn't come home after work. She said she had a million errands to run, which was why Billy was there. He ordered pizza, and we ate it in front of the TV. We were watching a baseball game when I heard sirens.

"Jeez," Billy said, grabbing the remote and pumping up the volume. "That's one thing I don't miss about this place. It's like living in a war zone or something."

There's a fire station a couple of blocks west of where I live, a police station a few blocks south, and a hospital a few blocks north. Fire trucks, police cars, and ambulances are always racing around, sirens blaring. I'm so used to it that I hardly notice it anymore. It's just part of the noise wallpaper.

Someone knocked on the door.

Billy muttered as he heaved himself up off the couch to

answer it. I felt sorry for whoever it was. It was never a good idea to get between Billy and whatever sporting event he happened to be watching.

I heard the front door open. Out of the corner of my eye, I saw Billy step outside. Then Bautista hit a home run, tying up the game. It wasn't until the next inning was half over that I realized that Billy had been gone for a long time. When a set of commercials came on, I went to the door to find out what had happened to him. I saw flashing lights up near Danforth Avenue. There was a crowd of people in the street. Then I saw Billy walking out of the crowd, coming back down the street toward our house. Two uniformed police officers walked with him. They stopped on the sidewalk and stayed there while Billy came up the porch steps and said, "I'm going to call Kathy." Kathy was Billy's girlfriend. "I'm going to ask her to stay with you for a while, okay, Mikey? I gotta go somewhere."

"Did they arrest you?" I asked. I couldn't think of any other reason why Billy would have to go with the cops, and why the two cops at the end of the walk looked so somber.

When Kathy came over, Billy whispered something to her. She looked like she was going to cry, and that scared me. Now I was sure Billy had been arrested. I wished Mom would hurry home so she could straighten everything out.

"You be good," Billy said to me. "Don't give Kathy any grief, okay?"

"Okay," I said. "What should I tell Mom when she gets home?"

"It's going to be okay," Billy said. He hugged me, which should have told me something. Then he went with the two cops.

CHAPTER ONE

FOUR YEARS LATER

"We're waiting, Mr. McGill," Riel said. *Mister* Riel.

It figured. Every time homework was passed forward for him to collect, he went through the pile looking for mine. When it wasn't there, he always said something—in front of the whole class.

I ducked down and rummaged through my backpack. If you ask me, I put on a pretty good show too. Before I straightened up, I slapped a 100-percent-panic-stricken look on my face, like, jeez, how could this have happened—again?

"Problem, Mr. McGill?"

Someone near the back of the class guffawed. I would have bet every cent in my pocket that it was Vin.

"Uh, I guess I must have left it at home," I said. Where was the Academy of Motion Picture Arts and Sciences when you needed it? Hey, guys, it's Oscar night, and I've just given the performance of a lifetime.

Riel wasn't impressed. "You don't live far from here, do you, Mr. McGill?"

"Couple of blo— " Hey, wait a minute. How did he know that? The guy had been freaking me out for the past month. He was new to the school and brand new to teaching, but he had acted like he knew me the first time he saw me, and he'd been picking on me ever since.

Riel glanced at the clock. He opened one of his desk drawers, took out a slip of paper, scribbled something onto it, and held it out to me. I stared at his outstretched hand.

"Well, come on," he said.

I stood up and glanced at Vin, who shrugged. I shuffled to the front of the class and took the piece of paper. It was a hall pass.

"We've got forty-five minutes of class time left," Riel said. "It shouldn't take you more than fifteen or twenty minutes to get home, get your assignment, and bring it back here."

I stared at the pass. He was calling my bluff.

"I could just bring it in next time," I said. "That'd be easier."

"Bringing in your homework when it's due would be easier, Mr. McGill," Riel said. "I'm giving you twenty minutes. And I guess I don't have to tell you what happens if you don't show up here before the bell rings."

I shook my head. No, he didn't have to tell me. I'd been around that dark corner often enough to know what lurked in the shadows. I glanced at Vin in the back of the room, then headed out the door and down the hall. I slowed down when I was out of sight of Riel's classroom. Now what?

I could go through the motions. I could walk home, stand on the porch for a couple of minutes, then walk back to school empty-handed. Or I could circle the block a few times. Or I could march back into Riel's class right now and confess. It would all come down to the same thing—I had no homework to hand in, and that was going to cost me a detention.

I decided to circle the block. Maybe inspiration would strike. Nothing's impossible, right? Maybe I'd come up with the perfect excuse. Like, my house was robbed and the thief trashed everything, including my homework. Or, my uncle got tired of nagging me to clean up my room, so he scooped up everything in it and threw it in the garbage. Hmm, that wasn't bad. Today was garbage day. There were empty garbage cans all over the sidewalk. And Riel didn't know Billy was a slob. Or maybe—

I spent the next fifteen minutes walking around, trying to decide whether to go back to school. And if I did, should I go back to Riel's class or should I wait and go to my next class? Right, like math was going to be more thrill-packed than history. If it were day two, if I had music or gym, maybe I'd have gone back. But to show up and get ragged on by Riel and laughed at by everyone else in the class and then top off the day by sitting detention, what was the point?

I walked up my street, right past my house, and kept

going until I reached Danforth. From there I headed west, trudging past dozens of bars and restaurants until I reached the Bloor Viaduct. I walked across it, over the Parkway and the river, and kept on hiking until I hit Yonge Street. Then I headed south to the Eaton Centre. I groped in my pocket. Enough for a Big Mac and fries. And when I went to work tonight, my pay would be waiting for me. Considering my financial situation, though, it would probably be a good idea to talk to Mr. Scorza about getting a few more hours.

» » »

I worked Friday nights and all day Saturday at a grocery store on Danforth. Box-boy/stock-boy/you-need-something-done-just-tell-me-boy. On Saturday I kept glancing up at the tiny, elevated office that perched in one of the front corners of the store. The glass was frosted so that it was hard to look in, but I'd been up there and I knew it was easy for Mr. Scorza to look out. The office was above the main floor, so he had a good view of the whole store, from the produce section to the left of the front doors to the dairy section in the back and all the aisles in between. I knew he was in there, too. I saw the boxy shadow of his body. I must have glanced at the door to that office a hundred times on Saturday, hoping Mr. Scorza would come out. If he did, I could check out what kind of mood he was in. If it seemed like a good one, I'd ask about the possibility of more hours. But Mr. Scorza didn't come out, not once in the whole day, which was unusual. Did that mean he was in a rotten mood? Would his mood get even worse if I knocked on his door during my break?

I decided to wait. I guess that makes me some kind of coward, afraid to go talk to the boss. But by the end of the day I'd bagged maybe five hundred sacks of groceries. My feet were sore. I'd been standing in practically the same place since I started at eight in the morning. Saturdays were always the worst. People just kept coming through, and they were all in a hurry. Some of them wanted their groceries delivered, which meant I had to pack them in cardboard boxes and staple order numbers on the boxes and carry them out to the delivery van. The rest of the people had to have their stuff packed in plastic bags. A lot of the bigger stores were strictly bag-your-own. The customers had to stand at the end of big metal counters and scoop their own groceries into bags. Some places even charged for the bags. But not Mr. Scorza. His place was too small to have customers standing around. And a lot of them came to the store because we delivered. That made Mr. Scorza's store special in the neighborhood. It also meant that he needed a lot of help around the place.

When my shift was over I took another look at the frosted glass. I knew he was in there. But the store was crowded. Everyone would see me climb those stairs, which meant that everyone would see me come down again, and if I didn't look happy when I did, everyone would know.

» » »

Vin and Sal were waiting for me out on the sidewalk. Sal was sucking back root beer from a can. An unlit cigarette dangled from Vin's mouth. The story he told everyone was that he was trying to quit. The real deal was that smoking made him sick. But cigarettes made you cool, according to Vin. Even better, he said, girls admired a guy who was trying to quit.

Vin—Vincent—Taglia is my best friend. I've known him since kindergarten. He used to steal my toy cars, right up until the day I hauled off and punched him in the eye. After that he stole other kids' stuff, and he and I played with it. Salvatore San Miguel is a newer friend. His family came here from Guatemala a few years back. Sal's dad was a university professor back home, only he got on the wrong side of politics and got himself arrested and tortured, according to Sal. Sal says the family had to run away in the middle of the night. They had to leave behind everything they owned. Sal's dad was so messed up by prison and everything that happened to him in there that he never managed to get his act together and start teaching again. He works nights as a cleaner in an office building downtown. Sal's mother has a job teaching other immigrants how to use computers. They get a lot of help from Sal's aunt, who came here a long time ago to go to medical school. She's a doctor now.

"What's up?" I asked.

Vin grinned but said nothing.

“He’s got a big night lined up,” Sal said.

“Yeah?”

“Yeah.”

I looked at Vin, who smiled again. As we walked down Danforth he told me about a girl he had met at a party at his cousin Frank’s place. Vin comes from a big family. He has a couple of dozen first cousins, and they all live in Toronto. They all seem pretty tight, too.

“She’s in a play at Frank’s school tonight,” Vin said, his eyes gleaming. “She invited me to come.”

“She probably invited everyone she knows,” Sal said. “You know, fill up all the seats so she can feel like a big success.”

Vin punched him on the arm.

“What about you?” I asked Sal. “What’re you doing tonight?”

Suddenly he didn’t look so happy.

“My aunt is having a party for my father,” he said. “It’s his birthday, and she wants to cheer him up. Probably it’ll just make him suicidal. One more year when he isn’t teaching.”

“Yeah,” I said. If I’d been a girl, maybe I would have given him a hug. Sal always talks about his dad like it was no big deal—yeah, my dad’s kinda nuts, yeah, he’s always reading books of Spanish poetry, always mumbling poems under his breath, so what? Sal’s dad is a short, wiry guy who has this strange, sort of haunted, look in his eyes, like maybe he sees things that other people don’t and those things are scary. But when Sal talks about him, what he says sounds like it's just life, just the way it is. Maybe that's what he really thinks. Except that if it is, how come you can always see these tight little lines at the corners of his mouth when he mentions his dad? And how come, when he says those things, he never looks you in the eye? Never.

"Great. While you two are partying, I'll be sitting home watching TV," I said.

"No Jen?" Vin said.

I shook my head. An old school friend of Jen's mother was visiting for the weekend. The friend just happened to have a kid Jen's age so, of course, Jen had to be there to entertain. If I knew Mrs. Hayes, she had made it clear that entertaining did not mean introducing the kid to me. But there was no point in explaining that to Vin, not unless I wanted him to go on and on about how I was probably missing out on a threesome, like that was something Vin knew anything about as opposed to just something he had read in a magazine.

We turned off Danforth and fanned out across the sidewalk. Vin was telling us about the girl again. She was fashion-model hot, Vin said. He'd met her at the party and she had flirted with him. Sal laughed so hard that root beer shot out of his nose.

"Yeah, right," he said. "Some model is gonna flirt with you."

"Hey, I'm telling you," Vin said. Either it had really happened, or he had managed to convince himself that it had. Maybe *he* should be trying out for a part in a school play. He definitely had sincerity nailed. The girl had hung around him all evening, he said. She'd danced with him almost exclusively.

"Yeah, right," Sal snorted. "You. Dancing."

"*Slow* dancing," Vin said. The dreamy look in his eyes was also convincing.

We were heading over to Vin's place when I heard a clattering sound. I looked across the street and saw a metal shopping cart crash to the sidewalk, spilling cans and vegetables and fruit everywhere. Mrs. Jhun was standing midway up the steps leading to her porch, one arm outstretched, one hand clutching the railing. She was staring straight ahead but didn't seem to be looking at anything. Then her whole body wavered like an unsteady pile of boxes that was about to topple over. I dashed across the street. I probably should have looked both ways first. A taxi honked at me and zoomed by so close that I swear I felt the door brush my arm.

"Hey!" Vin yelled after me.

I bounded up the steps and caught Mrs. Jhun by the arm. She was tiny. The top of her head barely reached my shoulder. I could have picked her up like a sack of groceries, there was so little to her.

"Mrs. Jhun?" I said. She was still staring out into space. I don't think she even knew I was there, and that scared me. Her whole weight rested against me. I can't be sure, but I think if I hadn't grabbed her when I did, she might have tumbled down the stairs right after her cart. "Mrs. Jhun, are you okay?"

She turned her head and looked straight at me. After a moment she said, "Hyacinth." Now she was really scaring me.

"Mrs. Jhun?"

She drew in a deep breath. She was still looking at me, but now her eyes came into focus. She seemed surprised to see me.

"Michael," she said. "What brings you here?"

I was totally confused. She was acting like nothing had happened.

"Your groceries, Mrs. Jhun," I said, nodding at the bags that lay scattered on her cement walk.

She gazed at them as if she hadn't noticed them there before. I glanced around the porch, spotted a chair, and dragged it over.

"You sit down, Mrs. Jhun," I said. "I'll pick up your stuff."

She sat without argument. I straightened the cart and began to gather up the food—cauliflower, broccoli, a lot of other vegetables that I couldn't name. Mrs. Jhun did most of her shopping in Chinatown. She also hauled her cart across town to the west end, to Little Korea. I picked up boxes of things—some of them pretty squashed—that had writing on them in a language I couldn't understand. Chinese, maybe. Maybe Korean. I set everything back into the cart.

"Too many groceries," Mrs. Jhun said as she watched me. "Too many steps. And too many years." I laughed at the last part. Mrs. Jhun was always talking about how she was old, but she didn't look that old. Billy says that's because Chinese people and black people don't show their age the way white people do. But if you heard half the stuff Billy says about Chinese people and black people, you wouldn't pay attention to his theory on aging.

"Your eggs are toast," I said. By the amount of goo leaking from the cardboard box, I guessed all twelve were smashed. "You want me to get you some more?"

She sighed at the yolky ooze on her front walk.

"Hey, Mike!" Vin called from the other side of the road.

"Your friends are waiting," Mrs. Jhun said. "I can manage the rest. Thank you, Michael."

I waved to Vin—wait or go, the gesture said, it's up to you. I carried everything into the house. Then I folded the cart and tucked it into a corner of the porch for her. It was only when I went back down the wooden steps that I noticed that one of them was broken.

"Did you trip on this going up?" I asked Mrs. Jhun. "Is that what happened?" It probably wasn't. She'd almost reached the porch when I first saw her. But a broken step—she could trip on it next time even if she hadn't this time.

"I'll come back after supper," I told her. I had nothing better to do. "I'll fix it for you." I didn't know everything there was to know about home repairs, but I knew the basics. For sure I could fix a broken wooden step.

"You don't have to do that," she said, which is exactly

what I expected. Mrs. Jhun never wanted to be a bother.

"You could hurt yourself," I said. "You sure you don't want me to get some more eggs for you?"

Mrs. Jhun smiled. "Eggs can wait," she said. Then she reached up and touched my cheek. Her hand was as soft as velvet. I knew what she was thinking without her saying a word.

"See you later, Mrs. Jhun," I said.

"Jeez, what was that all about?" Vin asked when I finally crossed back over the street again.

"And *who* was that?" Sal asked.

"She was a friend of my mother's," I said. "She's nice."

"Speaking of nice," Vin said. And he started talking about the girl of his dreams again.

CHAPTER TWO

Billy was sitting on the porch, drinking a beer, when I got home. Billy's on the small side, and skinny—mostly from not eating properly. His straw-colored hair was always flopping into his eyes. He had to shove it aside every few minutes with an almost permanently grease-blackened hand. The front of his jeans was also streaked with black, and there were black smudges on his T-shirt. The first time people met Billy, they always thought he was my big brother, not my uncle. He's only ten years older than me. He had been living with my mom when I was born and stayed with us until he turned eighteen, three years before Mom died. Mostly I thought of Billy as a brother, too—a big, messy, spoiled one. He was too lazy to bother much with being an authority figure.

I counted the empty beer bottles under his chair. "Tough day at the garage?" I said.

Billy's eyes were watery as he turned to look at me.

"You got that right, Mikey."

My stomach rumbled. I'd had a doughnut and a carton of chocolate milk for breakfast and grabbed a burger and fries at Square Boy for lunch. But that was hours ago.

"Did you go grocery shopping, Billy?"

He gave me a look that said, Are you crazy?

"You're the one working at a grocery store."

"Yeah, but you're the one with the money."

Billy shot me another look. "I wish!"

I sighed. Things weren't looking promising. Again.

"So, you eaten or what?"

"I'm not hungry," Billy said. "Besides, I'm going out. I'll grab something later."

Great. My stomach was growling. And if Billy hadn't picked up any food, and if he was going out anyway, that meant that I was looking at a can of Beefaroni or some soup for supper, or, if I wanted to venture beyond heating and into cooking, scrambled eggs. I went inside, remembering how it used to be on Saturday nights or, even better, on Sunday nights, when I'd blow into the house after a day of football or road hockey or bike riding with Vin. I'd barrel into the front hall and my mouth would start watering as I inhaled the smell of a chicken roasting in the oven or cupcakes cooling on a rack on the kitchen counter.

My mom was a terrific cook. She didn't make buckets of money as a bookkeeper, but one thing I never had to worry about was being hungry. In summertime she grew vegetables in the backyard. Only weeds grew there these days. She had a big freezer in the basement—empty now except for the plastic bags of ice that Billy liked to have on hand in case his friends wanted to party. Four years ago, though, it had been filled with vegetables Mom had grown and frozen, and with strawberries and raspberries from pick-your-own farms. She stocked up on chicken and ground beef whenever the stores ran specials. The same with bread. She made strawberry and blueberry and apple pies in batches and froze them. Boy, did I ever miss all that food. It sure wasn't the only thing I missed about her, but there were times when I would have given anything, anything at all, to be sitting down to her roast chicken and stuffing with homemade gravy, mashed potatoes, and peas.

Billy never cooked. His kitchen skills were limited to microwaving TV dinners and heating baked beans. Sometimes he even took them out of the can first. Sometimes he brought a girl home and sometimes the girl would cook something—maybe a batch of spaghetti and meat sauce or some fried chicken. But that was usually at the beginning, when the girl was trying to impress Billy. And usually the girl wasn't thrilled to find out that Billy was guardian to a fifteen-year-old nephew.

These days the fridge usually held more beer than food. But if Billy missed Mom's cooking, he never said so.

I opened the fridge. There was nothing inside. Well, nothing except a margarine tub that might or might not have any margarine in it, a carton of milk—I hefted it, it felt close to empty—a couple of wilted carrots in the bottom shelf, a half-full jar of strawberry jam (which only made me think of the freezer jam Mom used to make), a shaker container of parmesan cheese, a couple of grayish pickles in a jar that I knew for a fact no one had touched in months—maybe even years. Not exactly the makings of supper.

I closed the fridge and opened a cupboard. Sugar Pops. I shook the box. Half full. A jar of now-completely-scraped-out peanut butter. A box of crackers. And a bunch of cans—Beefaroni, baked beans, spaghetti, peaches (Billy loved canned peaches in heavy syrup a million times more than fresh peaches). Vinegar. Dried spaghetti. A jar of no-name spaghetti sauce.

I took out the spaghetti and the spaghetti sauce and put some water on to boil. Twenty minutes later, just as I was ladling sauce over a plate of spaghetti and getting ready to shake some Parmesan over it, Billy appeared, sniffing the air.

"Hey, that smells good," he said, hooking the plate out of my hand.

I served out another plate of food for myself, followed Billy to the front porch, and sat down on a folding chair beside him.

"You don't want to buy groceries, that's fine," I said. "Just give me some money and I'll pick up some stuff. I could make a meat sauce. Maybe some sausages. Or chicken. You like chicken, right? I can fry some for us, maybe make some mashed potatoes."

Billy grinned at me as he scarfed down his food.

"You're going to make some girl a nice wife one day," he said.

"Earth to Billy, get with the times. Men cook too. The chefs at all the best restaurants are men."

"I hate cooking," Billy said. He looked mournfully at his empty plate. "Anymore in the pot?"

I shook my head.

"Yeah, well, I'm going out anyway. I'll get something to eat later."

He set his plate on the porch and got up to go inside.

"Hey, put your plate in the sink," I called. Too late. The screen door banged shut behind him. A few moments later he returned, flipping the cap off another beer bottle.

"You seen the toolbox lately?" I asked.

"It's probably in the basement," he said. You asked Billy where anything was and he always said the same thing—probably in the basement. "Why?"

"Mrs. Jhun tripped on one of her front steps today. I'm going to fix it for her."

Billy made a sour face. "What do you care about that old woman for? Jeez, I bet she doesn't speak decent English yet. None of those people do." It drove Billy crazy when people came here from other countries and had the nerve to speak their own language. Everyone should learn English, he said. They shouldn't even be allowed in here until they could speak the language. To hear him, you'd think that learning a new language was the easiest thing in the world. Billy's only attempt to learn another language was the French that he had to take in school. Mom told me that he had failed it every year he took it. It was part of the reason he never graduated. The rest of the reason was that he had failed math, science, English, and almost every other subject that was required. Billy always said he didn't care. He always said he made a good living as a garage mechanic—which was why we lived in the palace that we did. He always said that one day he was going to have his own garage.

"She speaks English just fine," I told him. "And she was a friend of Mom's." Like I had to explain to him. "And I feel sorry for her."

Billy gave me another sour look. "Awww, you feel sorry for her," he said. "And why is that? Because her husband was a complete idiot?" Billy had a list of reasons for this opinion. Mr. Jhun should have called the police when he heard something in his restaurant instead of going downstairs to investigate himself. Mr. Jhun shouldn't have kept so much money around his place. Mr. Jhun kept a good luck charm near his cash register—that always got a big laugh from Billy. "A good luck charm in a dump of a place on this part of Danforth," Billy would say. "Jeez, doesn't the guy realize that all the really good restaurants are a couple of subway stops west of here?"

"The old lady's no genius herself, either," he said now. "She didn't even have the sense to stay with her own people."

"Shut up, Billy," I said.

"Aw, poor Mikey."

I stood so fast that I toppled the chair and stepped on the plate Billy had left on the floor. It cracked under my weight. I glowered at Billy, then kicked the stupid plate. It sailed out into the middle of the yard. When it landed on the hard-packed weed bed that Billy called a lawn, it broke into half a dozen pieces.

"Temper, temper, Mikey," Billy said.

I felt like decking him. Instead I went out into the yard and picked up the pieces of plate. Dan and Lew showed up just as I was about to dump them in the garbage can at the side of the house. Dan Collins and Lew Rhodes were Billy's closest friends. Lew worked at the same garage as Billy and had a thing for Marilyn Monroe—don't ask me why; she had died way before he was born. But that didn't stop him from worshipping her. His favorite T-shirt had Marilyn's face on the front. A plastic Marilyn key chain dangled from the rearview mirror in his car. He had no luck at all with real women, though, according to Billy. Dan was different. I wasn't 100 percent sure what Dan did. If you asked him, he'd just say "This and that," and flash you his movie-star smile. Billy said that Dan made out like a bandit with women on account of that smile. Women loved Dan, he said. Mom never had, though. I thought Dan and Lew were okay. True, you pretty much had to roll Billy, Dan, and Lew together to get a high school diploma, but they were doing just fine. All three of them had decent jobs, they made decent money, they could always find a party, and they were a lot of fun.

"Hey, Mikey, how's it going?" Dan said. He grabbed me around the neck and knuckled my head. He'd been doing that forever, and he always laughed when he did it. He looked at the pieces of plate in my hand. "When they say flying saucer, they don't mean that kind of saucer," he said. "Those babies don't fly at all, last I checked."

"Still in school, kid?" Lew said. He'd been asking me that for the past month.

"He's only fifteen," Billy called from the porch. "If he doesn't go to school, I'm the one who gets in trouble."

"Billy in trouble?" Dan said. "Been there, done that, huh?"

The three of them went inside.

I picked up my plate and Billy's empties and took them into the kitchen. After that I rooted around in the basement until, miracle of miracles, I found the toolbox. By the time I was ready to go, the guys were all on the porch again.

"We're going out," Billy said.

"You want to come with us?" Dan said. "I know this girl. She's got a kid sister. Really cute. Be just right for you."

"He's already got a girl," Billy said. He meant Jen. "And she's rich."

In unison, Dan and Lew gave me a thumbs-up.

"You're going to be cool, right?" Billy said.

He asked the same thing every time he went out. If I had said something like, No, I'll probably burst into flames if you leave, Billy would have done the same thing he did now. He grinned and started to turn before I could even nod. A split second later the door clicked shut. I sure wished I could have gone with them. I wished I could have gone *anywhere*, with *anyone*. Instead I grabbed the toolbox and headed over to Mrs. Jhun's house. On the way, I stopped at a hardware store to pick up a piece of wood.

» » »

Up until he was killed when he discovered a burglar in his place one night, Mrs. Jhun's husband ran a restaurant on Danforth Avenue five minutes from my house. It was one of those places that served Chinese and Korean food together with steaks and burgers—something for everyone. No matter which kind of food you ordered, the meals were always good. A visit to Mr. Jhun's restaurant was our end-of-the-week treat. By Friday night, Mom would say she was "all kitchened out." She'd change out of her work clothes, we'd walk up to Mr. Jhun's place, and Mom would order stuff like steamed vegetables and rice. I mostly stuck to chicken fingers and fries, although I had to admit, I liked what Mr. Jhun did with egg rolls and wontons. Mom was a bookkeeper—a job I didn't understand until after she died. I thought it was something like a librarian. Mostly she worked in an office downtown, but she also did work on the side to pick up extra cash. Mr. Jhun was one of her clients.

When I showed up at Mrs. Jhun's house with my tools and my piece of wood, she looked so happy to see me that I thought maybe she hadn't understood me when I said I was coming back. Or maybe she hadn't believed me. She looked a lot better than she had that afternoon. She insisted on making tea and giving me something to eat before I started working. That was fine with me. I liked the kind of tea Mrs. Jhun made, and she served it with walnut cakes that didn't just taste like walnuts, they were actually shaped like walnuts. She told me that they were like Korean doughnuts—everyone there ate them. I could understand why. They were delicious.

When I finally opened up the toolbox, Mrs. Jhun sat on a stool on the porch to keep me company. She watched me remove the old wooden step, measure and saw a new one, and nail it down.

"Where did you learn to do that?" she asked.

Where else? "Mom taught me." Mom taught me everything I knew about cooking, cleaning, and home repairs. My mom was that kind of person. Independent. If at first you don't succeed, try, try again. No retreat, baby, no surrender. And, third time's the charm.

I had a father, too. Some guy named Robert McGill. He and Mom got married a few months before I was born and stayed married until my first birthday. Mom didn't like to talk about him. All she would ever say was, "Your father was a restless man." Billy told me something different. Billy was eleven when good old Bob got itchy feet. One day, Billy said, Mom came back from the park with me and found all of Bob's clothes and his tape collection gone. Same with any spare cash Mom had stashed away. "He didn't like kids," Billy said. "He didn't like that Nancy had me to look after, and he especially didn't like a baby around that she had to take care of night and day."

I had never met my father and never wanted to. Then, about a year after Mom died, Billy got a letter from some lawyer informing him of the death of Robert McGill in what the lawyer called a single vehicle accident. They think he fell asleep at the wheel. If you ask me, he had been asleep at the wheel for a long time.

"How is your uncle?" Mrs. Jhun asked.

I shrugged. "Okay, I guess."

"He takes good care of you?"

I shrugged again. Mrs. Jhun didn't know Billy very well, but that wasn't her fault. She had tried. She had gone back to Korea after Mr. Jhun died. Then, about eight or nine months ago, she had returned. That's when she found out that Mom had died. She came over to our house to tell Billy and me how sorry she was. Billy didn't even ask her in. He made her stand out on the porch on a cold February afternoon. He listened to her, scowled when I invited her in, and looked relieved when she declined the invitation. After she left, he said people who talked the way she did should stay back where they came from. I don't know why he was so mad. She was just being nice, and besides, she spoke pretty good English.

While I worked on her step, she asked me about

school and told me that she was going back to Korea again soon for a visit. Mr. and Mrs. Jhun didn't have any children, but Mrs. Jhun had a sister and some nieces and nephews back there. One of her nieces was expecting a baby. She told me that she liked it there and she liked seeing all her relatives. But she also liked Canada. Besides, Mr. Jhun was buried here in Canada. He had tried so hard to make a life here, she said. She didn't think it was right to leave him here all alone. She said when she died, she wanted to be buried next to him.

"Don't talk about dying, Mrs. Jhun," I said. "You're way too young for that."

She smiled serenely. She looked so much better than she had this afternoon that I decided to ask her about what she had said.

"Hyacinth?" she repeated, frowning.

"You were looking right at me when you said it." Suddenly she smiled and nodded.

"Your eyes," she said. "They are exactly the color of hyacinth. Your mother's eyes were the same."

I felt a little better. It made sense in a Mrs. Jhun kind of way. It wasn't crazy. It reminded me of the time she said Billy had a mule on his head. I thought she got a word mixed up. Then she said, "He pushes it and pushes it, but it never goes where he wants it to go." And that was true. No matter what he did, Billy always ended up with his hair in his eyes.

"You remind me so much of your mother," Mrs. Jhun said. She smiled again, but there was something sad behind it. I knew how she felt. I felt the same way.

I stayed and drank another cup of tea with her, and promised I'd come back to see her again soon. Then I headed home to an empty house.

» » »

On Sunday I hung out with Vin. Then, when I was walking home along Danforth, I passed Mr. Scorza's grocery store. I stopped and doubled back. We were short of milk. At least, that's the excuse I gave myself when I went in. But as I was walking back to the dairy section, I scanned the aisles.

"Looking for something, Michael?" a voice said. It was Mr. Scorza, and he actually smiled at me. It was kind of a gruff, crooked, half-hidden-behind-his-moustache smile, but it gave me enough courage to say, "Could I talk to you for a minute, Mr. Scorza?"

"Sure," he said. "Step into my office."

I followed him up the narrow stairs and stood wedged in the small box-free area of floor space between the door and his desk, which was piled with invoices, bills, and shipping papers.

"What can I do for you, Michael?" Mr. Scorza said. He always called guys by their full names. I was Michael. Tom was Thomas. Steve was Stephen.

"I was wondering, Mr. Scorza," I began. All of a sudden my mouth turned dry and my tongue got tangled up in my teeth. I must have sounded like a kindergarten kid on his first day away from mommy, all nervous and shy. *Spit it out*, I told myself. *So what if he says no? It's not going to kill you, is it?*

"I have some extra time," I began, rushing the words out.

Mr. Scorza's eyes were fixed on mine. The smile had vanished from behind his moustache. I backed up a little without looking where I was going. My foot hit a box and I started to topple backwards. My hands flew out and I grabbed at another box to stop myself from falling, but the one I grabbed must have been empty or filled with feathers or something because when I grabbed at it, it lifted easily and I kept falling. Mr. Scorza started to get up from his desk. He looked worried. I sat down hard on the box behind me. Then, with him still watching and still not saying anything, I stood up and tried not to look like a major goof.

"Relax, Michael," Mr. Scorza said. "I don't bite."

I tried to smile. My lips trembled. It was too late to back out. I had already started.

"What I mean is, if you needed someone to work a few more hours, I'm available," I said. "I'm a hard worker, Mr. Scorza." It was true. I didn't spend any time out behind the store like some guys who said they were going back to the storeroom to get another case of peanut butter or margarine or whatever, but who slipped out into the alley for a smoke first. I never did that. I don't even smoke.

"I know you are, Michael," Mr. Scorza said. "You've

been working here how long?"

"Almost a year," I said.

"Ten months, two weeks," Mr. Scorza said. For all I knew, he was right on the nose. "I had to let Thomas Manelli go today," he said. "You know Thomas?"

Sure I did. Thomas was two years older than me and a real jerk. Where some guys would slip out for one smoke, Thomas would settle in for three or four, and he'd go on about how stupid Mr. Scorza was, how easy it was to put one over on him. *Guess not, eh, Tommy?*

"Thomas worked for me three days a week, four to nine. His shift is available," Mr. Scorza said.

I stared at him. "You mean, me?"

"If you think you can handle it."

"You mean, on top of what I already do?"

"If you think you can handle it," Mr. Scorza said again. "I like to see a boy get a good education. Your schoolwork is important, Michael. You don't want to let it suffer."

I nodded, but I wasn't thinking about school. Instead I was calculating how much more money I would make. Five hours a day times three days a week would add fifteen more hours to my paycheck. I'd have more money than I'd know what to do with.

"I can handle it, Mr. Scorza," I said. "I know I can."

"You can start Tuesday, Michael. Tuesday, Wednesday, and Thursday, right after school. Okay?"

"Okay," I said, and before I knew what I was doing, I had thrust out a hand. Mr. Scorza smiled at me as he shook it.

"Your mama used to come in here every Friday night and buy her groceries for the week," he said. "From the time you were this big." He held his hands barely a shoulder width apart. "She always had you with her. She would be proud of you, Michael, if she could see you now."

"Thank you, Mr. Scorza."

I was careful not to trip over any more boxes as I let myself out of Mr. Scorza's tiny office. And I had done it! I had asked for extra hours, and I had got them. Now I was going to be making more money, which meant maybe I could buy a couple of pairs of new jeans and some new sneakers, and I'd still have enough money left over to take Jen out.

» » »

I grabbed the cordless phone and carried it back to the living room, dialing on the way. It was stupid. It was like stepping up to the self-serve counter and asking for an order of trouble—supersized, of course—but I wanted to tell someone my good news. I flopped onto the couch and listened to the ringing on the other end of the line. Then:

"Hello?" It was a woman's voice. I recognized her right away—Jen's mom. Her voice sounded cold and suspicious.

"Can I speak to Jen, please?"

"Who is this?" she demanded. I never called Jen's house, and I was beginning to wish I hadn't picked up the phone now. Then I thought, *Where did she learn her phone manners, anyway?* I'd been nice, said please. She was snarling at me without having any idea who I was. One more thing that money didn't buy, I guess.

"I'm a friend of Jen's. From school."

"She's never mentioned anyone named Wyatt," she said, even though I hadn't said my name—which isn't Wyatt. That was Billy's name.

Then I realized that she had call display. Still, she had no right to quiz me. Jen wasn't a baby. She could decide for herself whether she wanted to talk to me.

"Look, is she home or what?" I said.

In the background I heard a man's voice. Jen's dad. A big-deal Bay Street lawyer. "Who is it, Margaret?"

"She's not available," Jen's mother told me. I imagined her smiling as she said it, looking like Cruella de Vil or Snow White's nasty, nasty stepmother.

Then I heard another voice, a female voice, say, "Who's not available?"

I wished I could shout over Jen's mother to get Jen's attention, but I couldn't. So I hung up. A few seconds later the phone rang. Jen, maybe? I pressed the on button.

"Who is this?" a voice demanded. Jen's mother again. "Who is this? Why are you calling my daughter?"

I hit off and didn't answer when the phone rang a third time. Jeez, how could Jen stand living with parents like those?

CHAPTER THREE

Mr. Morrison, my homeroom teacher, wagged a finger at me as I came through the door on Monday morning.

"Mr. Gianneris wants to see you in his office," he said. "Right now."

Mr. Gianneris was the vice principal. He motioned me into a chair as soon as I stepped into his office. I glanced at the picture of his wife and kids that he kept on his desk for everyone to see. I wondered what vice principals were like when they weren't at school, chewing out kids. Did they do a quick brain transfer at the end of the day? Or did they go home and chew out their kids the way they did everyone else? My personal opinion: Mr. Gianneris was like the dad in one of my mom's favorite movies, *The Sound of Music.* Line them up and march them to breakfast, Maria. After inspection, of course, and only if they pass.

He peered solemnly at me across his desk. It was

one of those moves that was supposed to make me sweat or confess or something. Then he opened a file folder, glanced at the contents, and asked me if I knew why he had called me down. When I said I didn't, he gave me his best vice-principal glower and said, "Really?"

I thought about giving him some wiseass answer, but what was the point? I was already in trouble. Jazzing Gianneris was only going to make him double whatever punishment he had already decided to dish out.

"This is about history class, right?" I said.

"Specifically, it's about ditching history class," Mr. Gianneris said. He glanced at the file folder again. "In fact, it's about ditching the whole day on Friday."

Blah, blah, blah. End of story: a week of detentions.

"Three-thirty to four-thirty, every day this week, Mike," Mr. Gianneris said, "starting this afternoon."

This afternoon was no problem. But what about the rest of the week? I thought about all the extra hours Mr. Scorza had just given me and about how he thought I was a hard worker. What kind of hard worker showed up for work forty-five minutes late because he'd been sitting in detention?

"But I have a job after school, four days a week," I said.

"You should have thought about that before you decided to take some unscheduled time off." Mr. Gianneris didn't even look up from the detention slip he was filling out.

It was decision time. I had three choices. I could suffer in silence, take the detention, and probably lose my job as a result. Of all the miserable luck. I could explain the situation to Mr. Gianneris, get down on my knees and beg, if that's what it took, make him understand exactly what was at stake and how important it was. The thought was humiliating. Mr. Gianneris didn't like me. What chance did I have that he'd give me a break? Or I could ditch the detentions, just like I'd ditched school on Friday. I'd probably end up suspended, which would free me up for work, but would kill my school record. I watched Mr. Gianneris fill out the slip.

"Sir?"

The word worked magic, like I'd said "Open Sesame." Mr. Gianneris looked up at me.

"Look, I know I messed up," I said. I worked at sounding sincere. It wasn't hard. This mattered more than almost anything else I could think of. "But I just got this after-school job, and I'm supposed to be there at four o'clock Tuesday through Friday. It's real important to me. I'll do the detention, Mr. Gianneris. Only, maybe I could do it for five Mondays instead. And I swear I won't ditch again. If I mess up one more time, you can do what you want. Okay?"

I stopped talking then and held my breath.

Mr. Gianneris peered at me for what seemed like days. At first I couldn't tell whether it was the fact that I had a job, or the fact that I was asking for a favor, that accounted for the look of surprise on his face. Then surprise gave way to suspicion. Finally I saw on his face the same look I had seen on Vin's face back in sixth grade health class, when we had started studying human reproduction—a look of intense curiosity.

"Where do you work?" Mr. Gianneris asked.

I told him.

"Tuesday through Friday?" Mr. Gianneris said.

"And all day Saturday."

"I can call and check, you know."

My heart raced. "The manager's name is Mr. Scorza. I've been working Fridays after school and all day Saturday for almost a year."

"Five Mondays in a row instead of every afternoon this week," Mr. Gianneris said slowly, as if he wasn't sure. Then he said, "A job is a good thing. It teaches a person responsibility." He studied me again. "Are you a good employee?"

Mr. Gianneris looked down at the detention slip he had just filled out. Then, finally, slowly, he crumpled it up and tossed it into the blue recycle bin near the door. He opened his desk drawer and pulled out another slip.

"You'd better not disappoint me, Mike," he said. "And I *am* going to check with Mr. Scorza."

I couldn't believe it. He had cut me some slack. First Mr. Scorza had given me more hours, and now Mr. Gianneris had made it possible for me to keep them. It was the biggest run of good luck I'd ever had.

"Thank you, Mr. Gianneris." I couldn't remember the last time I had thanked a vice principal. Probably never.

I spent the rest of the day looking over my shoulder, wondering what kind of trouble I'd be in with Riel on

Tuesday—or today, if I ran into him. I had a pretty good idea he'd be harder to deal with than Gianneris. I'm not sure why I thought that, but I did. I even thought that it might be a good idea to get that stupid paper done. Then at least I could wave it in the guy's face so that maybe things wouldn't go so bad.

But how do you find time for stuff like that when you've got classes all day and you leave every single one of them with another assignment and another deadline?

Okay, sure, I could have gone to the library at lunchtime and worked on that paper. Or headed straight home after my detention and stayed put until I'd produced the right number of words. But Vin was waiting for me like he'd promised, out in the school parking lot. He and Sal were going downtown and they wanted me to go with them, so of course I said yes. We were almost on the sidewalk when someone called my name. Jen. Vin rolled his eyes.

"So now I guess you're not coming," he said.

I shrugged and headed over to where Jen was standing. She had a pile of books from the school library under one arm. Out of the corner of my eye I could see that Vin and Sal weren't moving. They were waiting.

Jen's soft green eyes were as hard as emeralds. "You called my house, didn't you?" she said, like she had me on the witness stand and was trying to get me to admit to a major crime.

"Yeah," I said. "So?"

"Why?"

I had only met her dad a couple of times, but all of a sudden he flashed into my head. Jen looked just like him. Had his same crisp lawyer tone, too.

"I wanted to talk to you," I said. "What do you think?"

"You're not supposed to call my house."

Now I was getting flashes of her mom, too. Jen sounded like both her parents at the same time, telling me what I could and couldn't do. Like she had any right.

"I missed you," I said. "I just wanted to say hi."

"Yeah, well, my mom went ballistic. *Who's this Wyatt person? Why is he calling you?*"

"Did you tell her?"

"No!" Like that would have been the dumbest thing she could have done. It made me mad.

Okay, so maybe I hadn't met her dad under the best circumstances. But I had apologized for what had happened, and not just because I had to. I really was sorry. If I had known that bike belonged to Jen's dad, I never would have gone near it. And, anyway, I wasn't the one who took it. I just saw it. I noticed that it wasn't locked properly. A guy with a bike that cost that much should be a little more careful when he leaves it on the street. I just noticed that the lock looked funny, and I nudged it and saw that it wasn't locked at all. It was two other guys, older guys who were hanging around, who took it. They weren't even friends of mine. They grabbed it, but Jen's dad said I had helped them, so when they took off, I got in trouble. It didn't help that he never got his bike back.

It didn't help, either, that he could have bought himself fifty more just like it any day of the week.

But Jen didn't dump me because of it. She said she believed me. But she made me promise never to call her house. She said it would make her parents angry. Now, though, it sounded like she was ashamed of me or something. Why didn't she just tell her mother to mind her own business?

"Well?" Jen said. "Aren't you going to apologize?"

"For what? All I did was make a phone call—"

"We had company."

Jeez, why was she so mad?

"She grilled me for twenty minutes. I could see her friend was feeling uncomfortable. And poor Patrick was wondering what was going on."

Whoa! "Patrick?"

"My mom's friend's son. He just started at a private school here. That's why his mother was in town," she said. "I *told* you I had to entertain him."

"You said you had to entertain the friend's *kid*. You didn't say that *her* name was Patrick."

She went from pink to red in about one second flat.

"I thought you'd get all upset if you knew I was hanging around with another guy all night," she said.

She had that right. The worst part, though, was that she hadn't trusted me enough to tell me.

"Mike, I need my parents to relax a little," she said. "I don't need them to be watching me every second. You can't call me at home anymore, okay?"

"Bet it's not a problem if Patrick wants to call you," I said.

She answered by not answering. I didn't explode. I didn't yell at her. I didn't say anything. I just turned and walked over to where Vin and Sal were waiting. And, oh yeah, on the way there I plowed my foot so hard into the passenger door of a car, probably a teacher's car, that the car alarm started to bleat. That's when I ran. Vin and Sal caught up with me half a block later.

» » »

Billy wasn't home when I got there, but a miracle had happened. The fridge had food in it. Actual non-beer food. There was a package of hot dogs, with an eight-pack of fresh buns in a plastic bag on the counter. There was a loaf of bread, a container of coleslaw, a carton of eggs, an unopened package of bacon, a jug of milk, a couple of oranges, and a store-made apple pie. A note, in Billy's writing, was stuck to the fridge door. "Mike: Check the freezer," it said. I did. Squat in the middle sat a container of ice cream. Not the cheap stuff, either, but one of those premium ice creams. I couldn't help smiling. What Billy didn't know about nutrition would fill a cookbook. But he tried. Well, sometimes he tried.

I fried some bacon and then a couple of eggs. I set the eggs on a slice of toast, topped them with bacon, and pressed on a second slice. I put it on a plate with a generous serving of coleslaw and carried it and a big glass of cold milk into the living room, where I flipped on the TV and sank into Billy's recliner.

I had just eaten the last bite of my sandwich and washed it down with the last of the milk when someone knocked on the front door. Probably it was one of those gas salespeople or maybe one of those door-to-door religious types. But there was also a fraction of a chance it was Jen coming to apologize, which is what got me halfway to my feet. Before I got up all the way, I heard the door open. Good thing this wasn't a bank. I had forgotten to lock up. I hadn't even shut the inside door.

Someone called, "Hello?"

I set my plate and glass on the floor and poked my head out into the hall. When I saw who was standing in the doorway, I groaned.

"Well, well, Mr. McGill," Riel said.

"What are you doing here?" I said. What I was thinking was, Are teachers even allowed to do this? Are they allowed to just show up at your house? Wasn't there some kind of law?

Riel stepped into the hall and let the screen door clatter shut behind him, as if he'd been invited in, which he hadn't been.

"I looked for you all day, Mr. McGill," he said. He had a kind of lopsided way of smiling, but there was something behind it—and something in his eyes—that made me think he wasn't smiling at all, at least, not all the way. "You want to know why?"

I shrugged. I wished he'd go away. I couldn't believe he was even here, standing in my front hall, looking at me and looking all around at the same time.

"Apparently," Riel said, "it's not standard operating procedure at Eastdale Collegiate to send students home in the middle of the day to retrieve forgotten assignments. Ms. Rather and Mr. Gianneris—you know them, right?" Sure, I knew them. Ms. Rather was the principal. "They have this idea that if you send students—well, *certain* students—off school property during school hours and trust them to return, that you're pretty much giving them a day off. Apparently they frown on that."

"They give you a detention, too?" I said.

Riel grinned, like it was a fine joke. "Yeah," he said. "Yeah, something like that. They slapped my wrist, that's for sure." He looked straight at me. He never blinked, and his eyes never skipped away, not even for a split second. It was like he was staring right into me, or like he was trying to, and it made me want to look somewhere else, except that if I did, I was pretty sure Riel would read something into it, nervousness or cowardice, and there was no way I was going to let him do that.

"You have that paper ready?" Riel said.

Hey, wait a minute! Teachers couldn't just show up at your house after school hours and demand homework you owed them, could they?

"I, uh . . ."

"You what, Mr. McGill?"

Then there were more footsteps on the porch, and

Billy shouldered his way through the door. Dan and Lew were with him. So was Carla, Billy's current girlfriend, and some other girl I didn't know.

"Hey, Mikey, what's going on?" Billy said. He checked the expression on my face before turning to look at Riel. "Who are you and what are you doing in my house?" he said, puffing himself up so that he could feel taller than Riel, even if he couldn't actually *be* taller. Billy was average height and tried to make himself taller by wearing boots with thick heels. Even then, Riel had a big advantage on him.

"I'm one of your nephew's teachers," Riel said.

Hold on! How did Riel know that Billy was my uncle? Most people assumed he was my big brother.

"Yeah?" Billy said. "And?" He was looking closely at Riel now and frowning. If I didn't know better, I would have said that he knew Riel from somewhere, but was having trouble placing exactly where.

"Mike cut school on Friday," Riel said. "Did you know that?"

"No, I didn't," Billy said, his tone as somber as Riel's. But he turned and winked at me.

"Correct me if I'm wrong, Mr. Wyatt," Riel said. He also knew that Billy and I had different last names, only by now I wasn't surprised. I had it figured out. He must have gone into the school records. He must have read whatever was in my file. "But it's your job to make sure that Mike attends school regularly, isn't it?"

Billy had never liked it when my mom pointed out

his responsibilities. He didn't appreciate it any better when some teacher did the same thing. He took a step toward Riel. I think he was trying to appear menacing—or something.

"Look, Mr.—" He waited for Riel to fill in the blank.

"Riel. John Riel."

You could almost track the progress of the name as it entered Billy's ears—no particular expression on his face at first—then traveled along his nervous system into his brain. Bingo! The name got processed, and a signal went to Billy's eyes and the muscles around them, and to his mouth. He didn't look mad anymore. He didn't look like he was a hair's breadth from introducing the history teacher to the front door. Instead, he looked surprised. He leaned in to have a closer look at Riel. Then, slowly, he started to nod. Surprise gave way to amusement.

"Yeah," Billy said. "Now I've got it. Well, we've got things pretty much under control here, *Mr.* Riel, so thanks for your concern. Now, if you don't mind, I just put in a hard day at work, and I haven't had my supper yet." He nodded toward the door.

Riel didn't move. Instead he turned to me.

"What would your mother think," he said, "if she knew you were blowing off assignments and cutting classes?" He didn't wait for an answer, which was good, because I wasn't planning to give him one. "I want that essay on my desk first thing tomorrow morning, you got that?" Riel said. "If it's not there, *I'll* give you a detention—and I'll do it at my convenience, not yours."

Before I could say anything—and I wasn't even sure I was going to say anything—Billy ducked around Riel and opened the screen door.

"Okay," he said. "That's it. You're out of here."

Riel held my eyes a heartbeat longer. Before he let go he said, "I'll be expecting that paper." Then he turned and moved past Billy, not elbowing him out of the way exactly, but taking up so much space that Billy had to flatten himself against the wall to stay clear. Dan and Lew didn't move back as fast. In fact, for a few seconds, it looked like they were going to start something. They were a couple of big kids, just like Billy. Thought they were so cool. Thought they were so tough. Sometimes I just had to laugh.

Riel stopped. He didn't say a word, but he must have given them that steely teacher look of his because Dan and Lew backed up until they were outside on the porch. Riel loped through the door and didn't look back as he made his way down the steps and to the street. Billy watched him go. He chuckled when Dan and Lew came back inside.

"Thanks for backing me up, guys," he said.

Dan shrugged.

"They're not making teachers like they used to," he said. "That guy looks like he could really do a number on you."

Lew nodded.

Billy turned to me, shaking his head in admiration.

"Jeez, what kind of trouble did you get into at school

that they're sending teachers home to check up on you?" he said.

"He knows you," I said, "and you know him. How come?"

"He's a cop," Billy said. Then, "*Was* a cop." He laughed. "Jeez, the guy's teaching *school* now? What, phys. ed?"

"History," I said. "What kind of cop?"

"We still got some ice cream?"

I nodded and followed Billy into the kitchen. Dan and Lew and the girls went into the living room.

"What kind of cop?" I asked again.

"Detective," Billy said. "Homicide." He opened the freezer, grabbed the ice cream container, and carried it to the counter. "Heard he retired, though."

"Hey, Bill! Get your butt and some beer in here, will you?" It was Dan. He was always ordering people around. Always with a smile, though, so you actually wanted to do what he told you to do.

"Yeah, yeah, give me a minute with the kid," Billy called back. He scooped some beers out of the fridge. "Jeez, the guy's teaching school now!" He laughed as he flipped the lid off the ice cream and started eating it right out of the container.

"How come you know him?"

"You really don't recognize him, huh?" Billy said.

"Me? Why I would recognize him?"

Billy pulled another spoon out of the drawer and handed it to me. "Riel looked into things after Nancy died," he said.

I dug my spoon into the ice cream, even though I wasn't hungry. I didn't want to think about cops and my mom and the hit-and-run driver who had killed her and left her lying in the street, dying, then dead. And, no, I didn't recognize Riel. Didn't, or didn't want to.

Billy ate most of the ice cream, then grabbed some beers and carried them into the living room. Someone cranked up the stereo, ear splittingly loud. The party had begun.

I carried my backpack out onto the porch. Okay, so I could write my history paper or not write it. Besides history, I had some math homework, and my math teacher—I'd had her last year, too—assigned extra pages anytime you didn't hand in your homework on time. I also had a science lab to write up. I stared out at the tired-looking houses opposite ours. It was funny how streets were. Walk one block over and you'd see houses that were all painted up or had siding or brickwork that was well looked after. Turn the corner and the houses facing the park were bigger and had newer, more expensive cars in their driveways. But my little street? It was a down-and-out street where the paint was peeling, the porches sagged, and the grass looked crabby all summer. I told myself that I didn't care.

Riel wanted a five-hundred-word paper on the importance of immigration to the development of Canada. "All the information you need is in chapter two," he had said. "But don't even think about copying so much as one sentence directly. I spent my summer reading that book, people. I know every word in it."

Five hundred words. That was two full pages. I opened my textbook and tried to make myself concentrate. But all I could think was, Riel had been a cop. Riel had investigated Mom's death. He knew who I was because he had met me after Mom died. Maybe he had come to the house. He must have, if he recognized me. But I didn't remember. I didn't remember much about the days following Mom's death, except going to the funeral parlor with Billy. I remembered looking into the coffin, even though Billy hadn't wanted me to.

"You're going to give yourself nightmares, Mikey," Billy said. But I looked anyway, and so did Billy. He laid a hand against Mom's cold cheek. I didn't touch her. I just looked at her. It wasn't creepy at all. She didn't look 100 percent like Mom, but she looked enough like her that I had started to cry, silently at first, trying to be a man like Billy had said, until I realized that even though she looked like she was sleeping, she wasn't really. She was never going to open her eyes. She was never going to look at me again or kiss me or make fried chicken for me. Then, just like that, my shoulders started to shake and I started to sob—great, wracking noises that came from somewhere deep, deep inside and that made me shake and shudder all over.

I remembered a few things from after the funeral. I remembered how quiet it was in the house without Mom humming and rattling pans and running the vacuum cleaner. If there was one thing she couldn't stand, it was dust. I remembered how the whole smell of the house changed—no more fragrance of Mom's hand cream and face cream and cologne. No aroma of roast chicken or meatloaf cooking in the oven. No fresh pie smells or fresh cookie smells. I remembered how cluttered it seemed, too, without Mom picking things up and putting them back in the cupboards or closets or drawers where they belonged. I remembered Billy and Kathy going through all Mom's stuff, putting her clothes in green garbage bags, piling them into Billy's car and taking them to Goodwill. I remember Billy sorting through her dresser where she kept her special things—our birth certificates, her insurance papers, a picture of my dad, the little bit of jewelry that she owned. I remembered people coming and going. Kathy spent a lot of time at the house, until one night when Billy yelled at her—again—because she had showed up late when she had promised to babysit and made Billy late for some appointment he had. There'd been a big blowout that day and Kathy had never come back. I remembered visits from Mom's friends. Almost all of them brought food. I remembered some of them sitting in the kitchen with Billy, drinking coffee and talking in low voices, and I remember that Billy was always in a bad mood when they left.

"What do you think?" he said to me after one visit. "Do you want me to farm you out to some *decent* family, or do you want to stay with me?"

I was stunned that Billy had even asked. I had started to cry again, thinking that Billy didn't want me, and

Billy had teased me, saying if I kept on acting like a girl, he was going to send me to live somewhere else for sure. Then, I'm not sure why, he suddenly stopped kidding and he hugged me real tight—not a pal hug, like guys do sometimes, but a clinging-to-me hug.

"Hey, Mikey, I was just kidding. We're like brothers, right? I'd never send you away. Never."

Maybe there had been cops in the house, too. Maybe one or two or more of the nights when Billy had been sitting in the kitchen, drinking coffee and talking low, maybe he had been talking to a cop. But if he had, he never said anything about it to me, and they never found the guy who had run Mom down and left her in the middle of the street.

I stared at my textbook.

"What would your mother think if she knew you were blowing off assignments and cutting classes?" Riel had asked.

She wouldn't be happy, that was for sure. She wouldn't be happy about the way anything was going in my life—not the grades I was making, not the comments that accompanied those grades on my report card. *Needs to make more effort. Needs to complete assignments. Needs to pay attention.*

Yeah, but so what? She wasn't here, and I didn't care about school. It was stupid. History was history, who cared about it? What was I going to do with algebra and geometry? What did chemistry matter to my life? And what was the deal with French, anyway? It wasn't like

I was ever going to live in Quebec or in some French-speaking country. So what was the point?

Still, I didn't need any more grief. Not this early in the year. And, okay, so maybe I wasn't going to be a brain surgeon, but even I knew that you pretty much needed a high school diploma these days. I had heard that even the auto plants were demanding it. For some jobs, they wanted you to have more education. So maybe high school was like vegetables. "You don't have to *like* broccoli, Michael," Mom used to say, "but you *do* have to eat it." You had to eat it because it was good for you. You had to get through high school so that you didn't end up a shelf stocker down at Mr. Scorza's grocery store for the rest of your life.

So, fine, I read the stupid chapter in the textbook, and I wrote the stupid five hundred words, counting them carefully, throwing in a few *therefores* and a handful of *for this reasons* to get the right word count. I was folding the paper into my history textbook and reaching for my math assignment when I heard someone whistle. It was a distinctive whistle, like a bird chirping—a Vin whistle.

I spotted Vin and Sal down on the sidewalk. I ditched my math book and joined them.

"We figured you needed cheering up," Vin said. "Come on."

I glanced back at the porch. I thought about my math teacher and all the extra work she would load on me if I showed up without my assignment done. Then I heard the vintage Rush sounds that were blasting from the house. *Roll the bones. Take a chance.*

"Hang on a sec," I said. I ran up to the house and shouted at Billy that I was going out for a while. I don't know whether he heard me or not. Either way, he probably wouldn't have cared.

We headed down to the park first. There were quite a few kids there—big kids, kids from our school and kids from the Catholic school right next to the park. Some guys were shooting hoops in the dark. A bunch of girls hung out on the sidelines, watching, listening to music from a boom box, a couple of them were sort of dancing. There was another bunch of kids over on the playground—girls swinging on the swings, shrieking their way down the kiddie slides, a guy and a girl on a seesaw, him mostly keeping her up in the air.

We hung out there until a cop car swung down the road that cut through the park. The people in the houses facing the park had probably complained about the noise. They always did.

We followed a path that led under the railroad tracks and walked along for a while until we hit the 7-Eleven. Vin had some money. We bought some Cokes and headed back up to Danforth. It was nearly midnight, but none of us felt like going home.

"Hey," Vin said. He thrust an arm across my chest as he came to a stop. "Check it out."

It was a delivery truck. A bakery delivery truck parked on a side street just south of Danforth. The back of the truck was wide open. Vin approached it and peeked inside. I followed at a distance, glancing around to see if anyone was looking because, if they were, they might think we were planning to grab stuff, which we weren't. At least, I wasn't.

"Look at all that stuff," Vin said.

There were boxes of two-packs of cupcakes—chocolate, vanilla, strawberry swirl—and doughnuts. Packages of brownies and chocolate chip cookies. There were coffee cakes, lemon cakes, lemon tarts, butter tarts. There was angel food cake and devil's food cake. There were miniature apple pies and cherry pies and chocolate-coated chocolate cakes with cream inside.

Vin stared at the stuff, then backed away a few paces and glanced around.

"Where do you think the driver is?" he said.

What difference did that make? It was quiet on the street where the truck was parked and just as quiet on Danforth. Music drifted out from one of the bars down the street, but all the stores nearby were closed.

"Maybe he's taking a leak," Sal said.

Vin looked around again. Then, before I knew what he was doing, he jumped up into the back of the truck.

"Catch," he said, and threw a box of something at Sal. I looked around nervously. "Vin, I don't think—"

He chucked another box at me. I caught it by reflex. Cream-filled chocolate cupcakes with squiggles of vanilla icing on top. Supper was a distant memory by this time, and just looking at the cakes was making my mouth water and my stomach rumble. I could almost taste those squiggles of vanilla. But just to *take* the stuff?

Vin jumped down out of the truck with a third box tucked under his arm. "Come on!" he said as he ran down the street and ducked into an alley.

I glanced at Sal, who was looking in disbelief at the box in his hands. Then he shot off after Vin. I hung near the back of the truck for a moment, staring at all the boxes inside. Then, as I sprinted down the street, I told myself that no one would even miss what we had taken. Halfway down the block, a voice popped into my head. *What would your mother say . . . ?* It sounded an awful lot like Riel's voice. I slowed and threw the box over a fence into someone's yard.

Vin and Sal were way ahead of me. I turned on the speed to catch up. We wove through alleys and down side streets—"just in case," Vin called back breathlessly—before ending up in Vin's backyard to see what we had. Vin's box was filled with little single-serving apple pies. Sal had brownies. They both looked surprised to see that I was empty-handed.

"I tripped coming down Logan," I said. A lie. "I dropped it."

"Let's go back and get it," Vin said. "They were cupcakes."

"You crazy?" Sal said. "What if someone sees us?"

In the end, we didn't go back. We gorged ourselves on pies and brownies. Well, Vin and Sal did. I don't know why, but I had trouble swallowing.

CHAPTER FOUR

I took my history assignment to the school office first thing the next morning and asked one of the secretaries to put it in Riel's mailbox. Riel had it in his hand when he walked into history class later. He had read it and marked it. He came down the aisle and dropped it on my desk. D-minus.

"Would have been a solid D if you'd got it in on time," he said. He wasn't smiling, so I couldn't tell if he was being sarcastic or not. In fact, he wasn't even looking at me. Something outside seemed to have caught his eye. He walked over to the window and looked out. He stood there for so long that kids started to fidget and whisper. What was going on? Was the new teacher zoning out on us?

Finally he turned and walked to the front of the class. He opened a file folder, took out some paper, and started to lecture us about the settlement of Canada's west. It was about as exciting as watching wheat grow. There were no shootouts, no Indian wars, no cattlemen-versus-farmers conflicts, no Wyatt Earp or Billy the Kid. There were hardly even any guns. I was thinking about how best to position myself and my book so that I could take a nap when someone knocked on the classroom door.

Riel paused in mid-sentence. He crossed to the door and opened it. He stepped out into the hall for a moment. When he came back into the room, he beckoned to me. I glanced at Vin as I made my way to the front of the room.

"You're wanted in the office," Riel said.

Mr. Gianneris was standing in the hall. I tried smiling at him—he'd given me a break—but he didn't smile back.

"Come on, Mike," he said.

I looked at Riel, who just shook his head.

Mr. Gianneris didn't say a word as he led me down the hall and down the stairs. He showed me into Ms. Rather's office. She wasn't alone. There were two cops with her.

"These police officers want to talk to you, Mike," she said.

"What about?"

"I'm Constable Carlson," the older one said. "And this is Constable Torelli. Have a seat, Mike."

He waved me into a chair and then sat down opposite me. Constable Torelli stood to one side of me. He had a notebook open and was writing in it already, even though I hadn't said anything yet. Ms. Rather stood just inside the closed door, watching and listening.

I waited for an answer to my question.

"What grade are you in, Mike?" Constable Carlson asked.

I told him.

"You a good student?"

I shrugged.

"What's this about?" I asked.

"What's your favorite subject, Mike?" Constable Carlson asked.

Boy, I had to think about that one. Favorite and subject weren't two words I generally thought of in the same sentence.

"Music, I guess."

"You play an instrument?" He sounded like he really wanted to know, but I knew that couldn't be right. He hadn't come here to discuss my grades or interests.

"Sax."

Constable Carlson smiled. "You can get a nice sound out of a sax. You play in the school band?"

I shook my head. "But I was thinking of trying out this year," I said. It was true. Auditions were the week after next. I was pretty sure I'd have a shot at it.

"That's good," Constable Carlson said. "We want to ask you a few questions, Mike, about something that happened last night. A robbery. You don't have to make a statement if you don't want to. But if you do decide to answer our questions, anything you say can be used as evidence. Do you understand, Mike?"

They wanted to question me about a robbery? Jeez.

Stay calm, I told myself. Stay calm.

"We've asked your principal to call your uncle. He's your guardian, isn't that right?"

I nodded.

"You have the right to talk to a lawyer and to your uncle before you answer any questions, Mike. Do you understand that?"

I said I did. I noticed that Constable Torelli seemed to be writing all of this down in his notebook.

"Do you want to wait for your uncle, Mike? You can also choose to have Ms. Rather act in the place of your uncle, if you want. That way we can just clear this matter up right now. Would that be okay, Mike?"

I looked at Ms. Rather.

"It's up to you, Michael," she said.

"What do you want to know?" I asked.

"You want to tell me where you were last night, Mike?"

Stay calm, stay calm.

"Last night?"

"Yeah. What did you do last night, Mike?"

"Homework," I said. Which was true, up to a point.

"Where did you do your homework?"

"At home."

"Did you do anything else last night?"

I didn't know what to say. For sure they thought I had done something or they wouldn't be here. Had someone seen what happened with the truck? And how come they had just asked for me? Vin was in my history class. How come they hadn't dragged him down here, too?

"Mike?" Constable Carlson said. "What else did you do last night?"

What should I say? What *could* I say?

"Come on, Mike," Constable Torelli said. He didn't sound nearly as friendly as Carlson. "Make it easy on yourself. Tell us exactly what happened."

I heard a sound behind him, then a voice.

"What do we have here, fellas?" the voice said. I didn't have to turn to realize that it was Riel. "Are we questioning a witness or a suspect?"

Constable Carlson spun around. It was hard to tell who looked more surprised—him or Riel.

"John," he said. "I heard you were teaching school. Didn't know you were doing it here, though."

Riel half-shrugged. "He's a minor," he said. He meant me.

Constable Torelli stood up abruptly. "This has nothing to do with you, Riel," he said. He was right; it didn't. So what was Riel doing here? "Why don't you go back to your chalk and your blackboard erasers?"

"I believe we have the situation under control, John," Ms. Rather said.

Riel looked right past her and Torelli. He focused on Constable Carlson.

"If you're going to question Mr. McGill, first you have to inform him of his right to counsel and his right to have a parent present or any other adult he chooses. He has a right—"

"Relax, John," Constable Carlson said. "He's been

informed of his rights, and he has chosen to speak to us. Isn't that right, Mike?"

Riel turned to Ms. Rather.

"Did Mr. McGill specifically ask you to be here?" he said. "Or did you just offer?"

She shifted uncomfortably.

"We're going to handle this by the book, John," Constable Carlson said. "I just thought it would make it easier all round if we had a little chat first." Then he sighed, stood up, and touched me on the shoulder. The next thing I knew, he was telling me I was under arrest for stealing goods from a truck, and he was telling me again that I didn't have to make a statement or say anything, and that I had the right to contact a lawyer and my guardian. He kept asking me if I understood what he was telling me. The whole time he was asking and I was answering, Constable Torelli was writing furiously in his notebook.

Riel listened to everything that Constable Carlson said. If he was surprised that I was being arrested, he didn't show it.

"The most important part, Mike, is that you don't have to answer any questions if you don't want to," he said. "You understand that, right?"

I nodded.

"You want me to call your uncle for you?" he said.

"It's taken care of," Ms. Rather said. She didn't sound happy.

Billy wasn't going to be happy about this either, but

I'd rather deal with him angry than with everything else alone.

When they led me out of the school and put me in the back of a police car, I glanced up at the building and saw faces at the windows. Inside of five minutes, everyone in the whole school would know that I had been arrested. Jen would know.

» » »

Billy definitely wasn't happy about getting called away from work. He said missing time for any reason, especially a stupid-nephew reason, made his boss mad. The truth was, if Billy didn't show up late so often after partying hard the night before, his boss might have been more understanding. But I didn't think it would be smart to point that out, under the circumstances.

Billy didn't look comfortable walking into the police station. I didn't blame him. I didn't exactly feel right at home myself. They took us into the ugliest room I ever saw. There were no windows and no pictures on the wall. The furniture consisted of three chairs and a small table against one wall. They told me to sit in one of the chairs. Constable Carlson sat in another one, close to me. Billy sat to one side of me and a little bit back from me, so that if I wanted to look at him, I had to turn my head. Constable Torelli leaned against the table with his notebook open. They told me that they were going to videotape the interview. They told me again that I didn't have to answer any questions, but that whether I answered or not, I was still under arrest. Then they told me that anything I said could be used as evidence against me. They asked me again if I understood what they were saying.

"Shouldn't the kid have a lawyer?" Billy said. He sounded mad, probably because he knew that this was going to be a gigantic hassle that might end up costing him money.

"If you want to contact counsel, you're certainly free to do so," Constable Carlson said. He looked directly at me, not at Billy. "I have to tell you, though, Mike, that we have a pretty good eyewitness on this one."

Someone had seen us. I suddenly felt like I was going to throw up.

"What eyewitness?" Billy said.

"A shopkeeper in the area," Constable Carlson said. "He saw you, Mike. Gave us your name, told us what school you go to and where you live. Picked your photo out of your school yearbook."

I could feel the sweat sticking my shirt to my underarms. I tried to think how many shopkeepers knew that much about me. Quite a few, I decided. I had lived in the same neighborhood forever. My mom had shopped regularly at the same stores. She had even known most of the cashiers by name.

"This isn't going to go away, Mike," Constable Carlson said. "The company has been robbed before, and they're fed up. They're pressing charges. Why don't you just tell me what happened on Monday night?"

I felt like saying maybe they should tell their drivers to lock up when they left the truck, but didn't think the cops would appreciate the suggestion. I wanted to tell them that I had thrown the stuff away, that I hadn't eaten it. But what difference would that make? I had run with the box. Whoever had seen and identified me had probably seen me with the box. I had even choked down one of the pies Vin had taken.

"Maybe you shouldn't say anything," Billy said. "Maybe we should get some advice."

Constable Carlson looked at me. "You can call a lawyer, Mike. You can have a lawyer present when we talk to you. You and your uncle want to talk about it?"

Billy nodded and the two cops left the room.

"I just want to get this over with," I told Billy. "I want to go home."

"Yeah, but if we can get you off—"

"Billy, someone saw me. They gave the cops my name. How am I going to get off?"

"You can say it was mistaken identity."

"But it wasn't."

"Jeez, Mikey!"

When the two cops came back, Billy said we'd decided against a lawyer. They asked me if I agreed with what Billy said. I said I did. Then Constable Carlson asked me again what I had done last night.

"I did my homework." I said. "Then I went out for a walk."

"Where did you walk?"

I shrugged and stared down at the floor. "Just around. Around the neighborhood."

"What about that bakery delivery truck?" Constable Carlson said. "You want to tell me about that?"

There was no point in denying the theft. From what Constable Carlson had said, I had been nailed pretty good.

"We saw this truck," I said. "The back of it was wide open and, I dunno . . ." I really didn't know. Jeez, what had we been thinking? Why had I let Vin go in there? Once he was in, why hadn't I yanked him right back out again? When he threw that box of cakes at me, why hadn't I just thrown it right back into the truck instead of taking off with it?

"You dunno?" Constable Carlson said. He didn't sound mad or anything. Mostly he just sounded curious. "What happened when you saw the truck, Mike?"

"It had all these cakes and pies inside," I said. "We didn't think they'd miss a couple of boxes."

"What did you do, Mike?"

"We took a few things. That's all. We just took a couple of boxes."

"You and your friends?"

I nodded. I still couldn't look at him. I couldn't look at Billy, either. How could I have thought we wouldn't be seen? Vin hadn't even bothered to drop his voice.

"What exactly did you take?" Constable Carlson said.

"A box of cupcakes. A box of brownies and one of apple pies. But that's it."

"Three boxes?"

I nodded.

"You understand that by telling us this, you're admitting that you stole those cakes?"

"I understand," I said.

"Where can we find your friends?" Constable Carlson said.

I opened my mouth, ready to say, Vin should be in math class right about now, and Sal should be cruising into Spanish class—the one class he aced. Then it hit me. They wouldn't be asking me that question if they knew who had been with me. Whoever had identified me knew me, but either didn't know Vin and Sal or hadn't got a good look at them. So if I didn't say anything, the cops couldn't do anything.

"I don't know," I said.

Constable Carlson shook his head. He still didn't look mad. "I guess they're pretty good friends, huh, Mike? You don't want to rat them out, right?"

I stared at my feet.

"Look, Mike, if you didn't do this by yourself, why take all the blame by yourself?"

I kept my mouth shut. Constable Carlson sighed.

"It's your call, Mike," he said. "You don't want to tell us anything, it's up to you."

"I don't want to answer any more questions," I said.

I had to sit around some more with Billy, who was fidgeting by then. Finally Constable Carlson gave me a piece of paper and explained that I could go, but that I had to promise to show up at court on the date written on the paper. If I didn't show up, he said, I'd be in even more trouble. Then he gave me his card.

"If you change your mind about anything, you can call me," he said.

I tucked the card into my pocket and followed Billy out into the parking lot. He had a beat-up old Toyota that needed serious bodywork. When I got close to it I saw that Dan was already in the passenger seat. Lew was in back.

"You brought *them* with you?" I said. It was bad enough that I got hauled out of school by the cops. Did the whole world have to know about it?

"I told Gus I was too shook up to drive," Billy said, grinning. Gus was his boss. "Lew offered to help out. We ran into Dan. Besides, they're my best friends, and they're practically second uncles to you," Billy said. That was true. "And they're supporting me during this stressful time."

He opened the door and got in. I waited until the passenger door finally opened and Dan got out. He was shaking his head.

"Jeez, Mike," he said. "Busted? You actually got busted?" He slid into the backseat while I got in front with Billy. As I was buckling my seatbelt, Billy cuffed the back of my head. Hard.

"Hey!" I said.

"Stealing from a bakery truck!" Billy said. "What's the matter with you?"

"Yeah, Mikey, you're gonna get pinched, make it for something important at least," Dan said.

"I mean, going down for *cupcakes*!" Lew said.

He and Dan laughed. I was glad they found it so funny. Billy didn't, though.

"Nancy'd freak out if she knew," he said. He batted me on the back of the head again. "And if you don't want to give up your friends, don't say 'we' to the cops." He shook his head. "We did this, we did that," he said, mimicking me. "You got any brains in there at all, Mikey?"

He was still shaking his head as he turned the key in the ignition.

"What's going to happen now, Billy?" I asked as we drove home.

"You'll have to go to court," he said. "We should probably talk to a lawyer before you do. You should be okay, though. You've never been in trouble before. Well, except for that bike thing."

Jen's dad's bike. Jen thinks he pushed so hard on that because he's a lawyer. "It's the way he is," she said.

Jen's dad said he was in a coffee shop on the other side of Danforth at the time. He said he saw me remove the lock. He claimed I must have swiped the duplicate key from his house, which was the big reason I wasn't allowed to go there anymore. But he couldn't prove anything. And I hadn't done anything. Okay, so that included not trying to stop the guys from taking the bike. Maybe I should have chased them. Maybe I would have, too, if Jen's dad didn't always look at me the way most people look at garbage men in July—with their noses all wrinkled in disgust.

"Worst case, you'll probably get community service," Bill said. "But that's this time, Mikey. You do something stupid like this again and nobody's going give you a break. You understand?"

I nodded.

"What about V— "

Billy smacked me on the back of the head a third time. It didn't hurt, though. He was just trying to make a point. "Don't tell me anything more about it, okay, Mike?" he said. "If you don't tell me anything, I don't have to lie to anyone. As far as I know, you and *maybe* a friend of yours snatched some cakes from a truck—a stupid prank—and you're sorry and you've promised me you're never going to do anything like that again. Right?"

"Right," I said.

"Remember, you want to get along in the world, Mikey," Dan said, "you got to keep your nose clean."

"You listen to him," Billy said. "He makes sense."

» » »

I was supposed to report for work at Mr. Scorza's store that afternoon at four o'clock, but I didn't feel like going. So I hung out a couple of blocks from the place and waited until I saw another guy who worked there. Steve didn't go to the same school as me, but we talked sometimes at work and he was okay. I called him over and asked him to tell Mr. Scorza that I was sick.

"You don't look sick," Steve said.

"Just tell him, okay?" I said. "You ever need anything from me, just ask."

He nodded, but he had this look in his eyes, like, what kind of coward would ask someone else to lie for him? The perfect end to a perfect day.

CHAPTER FIVE

I always feel like the only white guy in Harlem when I head north behind the Carrot Common. The houses are a lot bigger there than they are where I live. Most of them have been restored or renovated, and all of them are well maintained. No paint peeling around the windows. No iffy patches of shingles on the roof. No moss growing in the gutters. No weeds sprouting in the lawns. No lawns at all in front of some of those places, just gardens full of flowers and shrubs and miniature trees trimmed into perfect little balls. The cars are as upscale as the houses—Jeeps and Beemers and Lexuses. It's not just that, though, that makes me feel like I don't belong. It's also the way the people look. The women's hair is always neatly trimmed. Everyone's jeans—kids' and adults'—are freshly washed and pressed. Their sneakers are always the latest styles and the best brands—Adidas, Nikes, Reeboks. Sure, they all talk a line about how a lot of stuff was made by ten-year-olds in Bangladesh or India. I bet half their kids had even done projects on the evils of child labor. But drop a bundle on shoes some poor kid had slaved to make? No problem.

The day after I got busted, I walked along the tree-canopied streets, conscious of the nicks in the sneakers I had bought at Payless. My jeans were frayed at the cuffs and the denim was thin in places. Any day now the fabric would rip and my knees would show through. Nobody stopped and stared at me, though. Nobody seemed to be wondering, What's *he* doing here? But I sure felt it. Around me—money. In the pockets of my worn-out jeans—no money.

A couple of blocks north of Danforth, I hung a left. A block later, a right. I slowed my pace and hung back at the corner of a hedge, just out of sight of the biggest house on the street. I could have looked at that house forever. It was five times the size of our place and was built of gray stone. It had a tower in one corner, and I knew from all the time that I had stared through the windows that the tower room—the library, Jen called it—was filled with bookshelves and books. The house also had a games room—they really called it that—with a regulation-sized pool table, a pinball machine, a Ping-Pong table, and an oak card table with special chairs. Her mom played bridge. Her dad had monthly poker nights with a bunch of other lawyers. A satellite dish sat on the tile roof. Two BMWs sat in the driveway, keeping an SUV company.

I watched the house while doing my best not to be spotted. I knew guys who came up here sometimes to swipe bikes—expensive bikes—that kids sometimes left unguarded and unlocked on porches or in open garages. I knew other guys who talked about getting into the houses themselves, but that's all it was, talk, because most of the places were on security systems. I sure would have liked to get inside some of those places, though, just to see what they kept in there. Check out the big-screen TVs and the bathrooms that were as big as most of the living rooms on my street. Check out the real live Martha Stewart décor, too, just for laughs. Maybe even see a nanny or a cleaning lady at work.

I saw a flash—sunlight reflected off glass so clean that it looked like it wasn't even there. The front door opened, and a man stepped out. He was wearing a gray business suit and clutching a briefcase. He stood on his stone stoop, surveying the neighborhood. I ducked to avoid being spotted. Why didn't he just climb into his black Beemer and go? What was he waiting for? Then a woman came out and handed him a package. He planted a kiss on her cheek—it didn't look very loving, if you ask me. The woman went back inside. I checked my watch.

I pressed a little closer to the hedge, turned my back to the street and ducked down—the old tie-the-shoelace trick—when I heard the Beemer's engine purr.

"You there!" said a sharp voice behind me. "What do you think you're doing?"

If I closed my eyes, I could imagine Jen's mother. But it wasn't Jen's mother who had said that. It was Jen, kidding around. That meant she wasn't mad at me, which put me in a better mood.

"Ha, ha!" I said. I wrapped my arms around her and kissed her on the mouth. She giggled halfway through the kiss, which most guys wouldn't have appreciated, but I took it as another good sign. Then she pulled away and glanced nervously back at the house.

"Mom's home," she said. "She's heard the whole story."

I wanted to ask how she had heard, but figured the message had probably been passed through the mom network and not through Jen. Jen never mentioned me to her parents—out of sight, out of mind.

"It was stupid," I said. "I don't even know why I did it."

Jen's green eyes widened in surprise.

"You mean, it's *true*?" she said. It took a moment for her astonishment to sink in. Jen had thought I was innocent. Maybe she'd even argued the point with her mother. And now here I was telling her the opposite. "You really stole from that truck?"

I had been embarrassed when the two cops took me out of the school and I saw kids watching at the windows. I felt stupid when Billy showed up, all mad because he had to take time off work on my account. But now I was ashamed of myself. I knew Jen spent a lot of time trying to convince her parents that I was okay. I could imagine her doing the innocent-until-proven-guilty thing with them at the dinner table last night. So I told her that I had tossed my box a block from the truck.

"You shouldn't have taken it in the first place," she said. She looked and sounded exactly like her mother. But she was right, that was the thing. I didn't argue with her. I agreed with her. She liked that.

"So, what's going to happen?" she said. She started walking slowly and waited for me to fall into step beside her.

I told her about my court date and about what Billy had said. I didn't tell her how it had all started—how Vin and Sal had just been trying to cheer me up about good old Patrick. I didn't tell her, either, that Vin and Sal had been in on it with me and that I had refused to give them up. I didn't think she'd find that as admirable as Billy had.

I spotted Vin almost as soon as I got to school. He was at one end of the parking lot, leaning against a lamppost. He must have been looking for me, because he immediately shoved himself off the post and started toward me. When Jen saw him coming, she said, "See you later." Her voice wasn't exactly ringing with anticipation, and I started to think about Patrick again. I don't know what she had thought of him on Saturday night when she'd been entertaining him, but I'd have bet a month's wages that he was looking pretty good to her right now. I bet he'd never done anything as stupid as getting arrested for stealing cupcakes. Bet he never would, either.

Vin came up to me, but he didn't talk to me. He didn't even stop walking when he got close. Instead he acted like a spy or an undercover cop. He walked right by me, and as he passed I heard him say, "Backstage after homeroom."

I didn't ask what the matter was. I didn't have to. After ten years, Vin's paranoid mind was no mystery to me. I figured he was afraid the cops were watching, which didn't make much sense to me. Sure, the bakery company was going to press charges, but we had stolen pastries, not money or audio equipment. Still, maybe if Vin was the one who had been nailed and I was the one who was worried about what the cops thought or what they had found out, I would have acted the same way. So I didn't talk back to him. Didn't even look at him. I just met him backstage like he asked.

The place was deserted. The auditorium is used for public meetings, concerts, the annual school play, and assemblies. The rest of the time, it fills up with dust.

"What'd you tell them?" Vin asked after he checked to make sure there was no one around. He didn't ask me how it had gone or what had happened. He didn't even ask what the cops were going to do to me.

"Nothing," I said.

"How come they knew to arrest you?"

"Someone saw me. Whoever it was knew my name, where I live, and what school I go to—the cop who arrested me called it a positive identification."

"Yeah, and?"

"And they know it was me. They know I wasn't alone. But they don't know who was with me."

"No one saw me?"

I noticed that he said *me*, not *me and Sal*. Guess it was every man for himself now.

"If they did, they must not have recognized you."

From the look on his face, you'd have thought Vin had just scored big-time with that girl who looked like a model.

"And you didn't tell them anything?" he asked.

"Jeez, thanks a lot!"

"Okay," he said. "Okay, just asking, that's all. So now what?"

I filled him in. I felt like I'd told the story a hundred times already.

"And you're not going to give us up?"

"All the stuff you've done, Vin, have I ever given you up?"

Vin slapped me on the back. "You're okay, Mike."

I kept my mouth shut. Maybe the cop was right. Maybe I was an idiot to be taking all the blame for something that I hadn't done alone. But what was the point of Vin and Sal getting busted with me? It wasn't going to teach them anything they didn't already know. And it wasn't going to change the fact that I had been caught more or less red-handed.

» » »

Everyone knew what had happened, which meant that I got the full eyeball treatment all day. Everybody had to look at the no-brains who'd put his personal freedom on the line for a carton of cupcakes. A couple of guys kidded me about it. None of my teachers said anything, but the ones who had already pegged me as a loser seemed to be congratulating themselves for their character-judging skills, while the few who had been willing to believe I wasn't all bad just shook their heads and looked at me with disappointment in their eyes.

Riel didn't say or do anything. He glanced at me when he passed me in the hall that morning, but that was it. I breathed a sigh of relief when he was out of sight. I guess because now I knew he used to be a cop, I thought he was going to chew me out. Turns out he didn't care one way or the other.

That afternoon I headed for work. I was even looking forward to it. It would be a nice change from school, where the major topic of conversation was how stupid I had been.

Melissa, one of the cashiers, smiled at me when I came through the door. Eileen, who was old enough to be my grandmother, said, "Hey, Mike. Hope you're feeling better." I told her I was, then coughed to prove that I really had been sick. I headed to the back of the store to pick up my apron—we all had to wear green aprons with the store logo and our name badge on them. On the way down the cereal and baking goods aisle, Mr. Johnson, the assistant manager, stopped me.

"Mr. Scorza wants to see you," he said.

My stomach did a backflip. I knew Mr. Scorza liked me. I also knew that he had been operating this store for longer than I had been alive. He knew all the other storeowners on this part of Danforth. I remembered what Constable Carlson had said—I had been positively identified by a local shopkeeper. With my luck, it would turn out to be a friend of Mr. Scorza's.

I went to the front of the store and knocked on the door to Mr. Scorza's office.

"Come in," he said, his muffled voice deep and ominous, like the rumble of an avalanche.

I opened the door and made my way up the little flight of stairs about as enthusiastically as most people would navigate through a minefield. Over the piles of boxes at the top of the stairs I saw Mr. Scorza's face. He looked at me and nodded, but he didn't smile.

"You wanted to see me, Mr. Scorza?"

"Come in and sit down, Michael," he said.

Sit down? Mr. Scorza's office was so crowded that the only chair in it was the one behind his desk, and the only person who got to sit in that was Mr. Scorza. But as I got closer, I saw that he had crammed another chair into the tiny patch of uncluttered floor space in front of his desk.

"I'm going to come right to the point," Mr. Scorza said. I could feel sweat under my arms. My palms were damp. Good news never followed an introduction like that. "It was a hard thing to have to do, Michael," he said. "A very hard thing. But what choice does a man have? You see something happen, you can't pretend you didn't see it. A person breaks the law and you see him and you say nothing, that's the same as breaking the law yourself."

I had grabbed a slice of pizza in the school cafeteria for lunch and had washed it down with a can of Coke. That was hours ago. It should have settled by now. But as I sat on that rickety chair listening to Mr. Scorza, I was pretty sure it was going to come up again. Up and all over my shoes.

"I believe in leading an honest life," Mr. Scorza said. "I believe in obeying the law. I believe in doing the right thing. So on Monday night, Michael, when I saw you steal things from that truck and then run away, what could I do?" He looked right at me. "I called the police."

Mr. Scorza had turned me in.

"I always trusted you, Michael," he said. "It never occurred to me not to trust you. Maybe this is because of what happened to your poor mother. You'll excuse me if I say that your uncle does not have the same character as his sister. So maybe part of the fault is his. But you're fifteen years old, Michael. Almost a man. And that wasn't your uncle out on the street on Monday night. That was you. You and your friends. So you have to take responsibility for what you did."

I thought about telling him I had already confessed. But I didn't because the truth was that I had confessed only after I had been positively identified—by Mr. Scorza.

"You have to pay the price for what you did," he said. "Deciding on that price is mostly out of my hands. It's up to a judge to decide how you should be punished for what you did."

"I'm really sorry, Mr. Scorza," I said. I was sorry that I had done it, I was sorry that he had seen it, I was sorry that he had called the cops. I don't mean I wished he hadn't called them, either. I was just sorry that I had made him do it. He looked almost more upset than me.

"I'm sorry, too, Michael," he said. "But I need to know that I can trust the people I work with. I couldn't trust Thomas because he was always taking too many breaks when he should have been working hard for the money I paid him. And I can't trust a thief working for me."

No. I could feel my head shaking involuntarily. *Please, no, don't do this.*

"I'd never steal from you, Mr. Scorza."

He looked sternly at me. "You only steal from strangers, is that it, Michael?"

"I don't steal at all," I said. "I mean, I just did it once, and it was stupid. I don't even know why I did it. But I swear it'll never happen again, Mr. Scorza."

"I hope it won't, Michael," he said. When he said that, I thought he was going to give me a second chance. "But what you did was wrong. What you did makes me wonder if I can trust you, and I don't like to work with people I have to wonder about. More importantly, I don't think it would be a good message to give you—that you can steal and not have to live with the consequences. I'm sorry, Michael, but I'm going to have to let you go."

My eyes started to burn. I felt like a little kid, fighting back tears.

"Please, Mr. Scorza, I need this job. I *want* this job. I like working here."

He crossed his hands over his chest.

"I have nothing more to say, Michael."

I don't know how I got down those stairs, but I did. When I got home, Billy wasn't there. I went into the living room, flopped down on the couch, and flicked on the TV. Don't ask me what I watched. I wasn't paying attention. Then I couldn't stand it anymore, just sitting there, doing nothing. I grabbed my jacket and headed down to the park.

All the little kids had gone home, and the park was quieter than usual. I climbed to the top of the slide and sat there, my feet dangling from the platform, thinking how disappointed Mr. Scorza had looked and wondering how soon I would be able to find another job. It was already dark when I noticed a guy jogging through the park. I didn't pay any attention, though, until it was too late. Riel. In a T-shirt and sweatpants. Looking up at me.

"Don't tell me I forgot to give you homework," he said.

I looked away from him.

"How'd it go with the police?" he said.

I shrugged. The message I was trying to convey: Go away.

"I did a little grocery shopping today," he said. "Had a chat with a cashier named Eileen. Nice lady. You know her?"

I didn't answer.

"She told me you got fired," he said.

Good old Eileen.

"What happened?" he said.

"I don't want to talk about it."

He shrugged. "Don't talk, then," he said, looking up at me. "Just listen. From what I've heard, you admitted you did it. You're going to have to go to court. You're going to have to tell the judge something. As it stands, you could be in for some trouble. You were seen with two other boys, but you won't tell the police who they are. That doesn't matter to the police, Mike. They aren't stupid. But it could matter to you and to a judge. Then there's that incident with the bike." He knew about that, too? "If I were the judge, I might think you weren't sorry. I might want to take steps to make sure you felt sorry. And with your home life and your uncle's character—"

"What about Billy's character?" I said. Who did he think he was, criticizing Billy? "Billy looks after me."

"Does he? Is he home now? Does he have any idea where you are?"

I didn't answer.

"He's not home a lot of nights, is he?"

"I'm not a kid."

"You're a minor. A minor in trouble with the law. A judge will want to know that a boy like you is being properly supervised."

"What do you mean, a boy like me?"

"A boy who steals and covers up for his friends."

That did it. I started to climb down the slide. Riel blocked my way.

"That's what the judge is going to see, Mike. That, and a guardian who doesn't act much better. The judge could decide that you need a little closer supervision."

"That won't happen!"

"Won't it? You sure about that?"

"You're just trying to scare me."

Riel shook his head slowly. "Maybe you should be scared," he said. "You barely passed any of your subjects last year, and you're not off to a very good start this year. You got yourself arrested, and you've lost the trust of a man who has always considered himself your friend."

He meant Mr. Scorza.

"You really want to end up like your Uncle Billy, Mike? You think that's what your mother would have wanted for you?"

"Shut up about her!" I yelled the words at him. You should have seen the stunned look on his face. "You talk about my mother like you knew her. But you didn't know her. And you didn't care about her. You didn't even bother to find out who killed her."

He stepped back a pace to let me down.

"We investigated the case thoroughly," he said.

"You gave up on it, you mean."

Riel stiffened. I guess he didn't like being called a quitter.

"Sometimes things don't work out the way you hope," he said.

"You mean, sometimes it's just not important enough to care about."

He looked at me blankly.

"Sure, deny it," I said. "But a couple of weeks after my mother died, those rich old people up in Forest Hill were shot in their driveway. Every cop in the city was on that case for months. They didn't quit until the found the killers." Billy had told me all about it. "And there was that girl who was murdered in High Park. The cops didn't give up on her, either. But then, her dad was the president of one of the big banks. But my mom gets run over and it's no big deal, right? Because my mom wasn't rich and she didn't have any big-deal relatives. Guess the cops don't care so much about nobodies."

For a moment Riel was silent. Then, in a quiet voice, he said, "I'm sorry if you think that's the way it happened. But it isn't."

"Leave me alone."

"Mike—"

But by then I had taken off. I was running across the park, away from him and the memory of my mother and the truth in what he had said. What would she have thought about the way my whole life was going?

CHAPTER SIX

I woke up in the middle of the night, bang, just like that. *You were seen with two other boys, but you won't tell the police who they are. That doesn't matter to the police, Mike. They aren't stupid.* Why had Riel told me that? What did he mean, That doesn't matter to the police? If it didn't matter, why had they pressed me for an answer?

It didn't matter because they weren't stupid.

I checked my clock. Three in the morning. Not the time to be calling anyone who didn't have his own phone line. Not the time to be waking up anyone's parents, either, especially not to say you had to talk to their son right now, it's an emergency.

I didn't sleep well, which made it easy for me to get up early. I skipped my shower, dressed, and went straight to Vin's house. When I got there, I hesitated. Should I knock on the door or just wait? There wasn't much chance he had left already—once in a blue moon Vin got to school before me. His parents were probably still home, not that it was such a big deal. I was Vin's best friend. I was always knocking on his door. True, I didn't usually do it at quarter to eight in the morning. But, hey, I'd done stranger things.

I climbed the front steps and knocked. Vin answered. He didn't look happy to see me, and that didn't make me feel good. Then he looked past me and said, "I thought we were friends."

What?

I watched his shoulders slump, then I turned and saw what he had seen. A cop car was parked at the end of his walk and two cops were getting out of it. Constables Carlson and Torelli.

"It wasn't me," I said to Vin.

"Hey, Mike," Constable Torelli said, smiling as he came up the walk. "How ya doin'?"

"I swear, Vin, it wasn't me." I wanted to tell him I had come over to warn him, but the two cops were right behind me now, and Constable Carlson was asking Vin if his mother or father was home.

Constable Torelli slapped me on the back. "Shouldn't you be running along to school?" he said.

» » »

I went to school because, to be honest, I was afraid not to. I hated to admit it even to myself, but the fact was, Riel had scared me. I thought about going to court. I thought about the impression Billy would make, even supposing he cleaned himself up and maybe scrounged a jacket and tie from somewhere. He didn't have anything like that hanging in his closet. I thought about my dismal school record and how it would look if I started cutting classes now. So I went and I sat in history and math and science. I blew my saxophone in music and hit a lot of wrong notes. I didn't care. Vin didn't show up in school all day. I looked for Sal, but I didn't see him around, either.

"You okay?" a voice said.

I was sitting on the stairs that led up to the stage in the school auditorium. It seemed safe enough there. At least, it had been until I heard the voice and looked up and saw that it was Riel.

"Yeah, sure. I'm great," I said. "Vin got busted."

"First thing I would have done if I was Carlson would be ask around," Riel said. "Ask the principal, ask the vice principals, maybe ask a few teachers—who does McGill hang around with? Who's he tight with? It's Police Work 101."

"Maybe. But Vin thinks I gave him up."

Riel sat down on the steps beside me. "Think it through for half a minute and it seems to me he doesn't have much to complain about. A, you didn't give him up, and, B, he was there, he participated."

I hadn't expected him to understand, and he hadn't disappointed me.

"Did Carlson ask you?" I said. Riel used to be a cop. He knew Carlson. I was in his history class. Wouldn't

Carlson have asked him if he knew who I hung out with? Wasn't that Police Work 101, too? And wouldn't Riel have answered?

"Yeah," Riel said. "He asked."

"And?"

"I'm new around here, Mike," Riel said. "There's—what?—fifteen hundred kids in this school? For someone as new to the job as me, this early in the year, it seems like they've all passed through my classroom at least once. It's hard to keep all the faces straight, let alone know who's hanging with who." He sounded like he meant it. I wondered if Carlson had believed him. "Mike, I want to talk to you about something."

"What?"

"Your mother."

He looked even more serious than he usually did in class. I waited.

"You were just a kid the last time I saw you, but you're not a kid anymore," he said. "I want to explain something to you."

He waited a moment and then went on. "I was in charge of investigating the accident," he said.

Tell me something I don't know.

"There's a standard procedure we follow in Traffic Services when there's been a hit-and-run."

"Traffic Services? I thought you were Homicide," I said.

"I transferred," he said. "Then I was in the Detective Office in Traffic Services."

Traffic Services. It sounded like parking tickets and traffic jams—nothing important.

"The first thing we do in a case like this," Riel said, "is try to locate any witnesses and see if they can give us a description of the suspect vehicle, or a description of the driver, or anyone else who might have been in the car or can tell us what direction it was traveling in. Then, the way it's supposed to work, whatever information we get, we pass along to the dispatcher and they alert patrol cars in the area."

The way it's *supposed* to work—which meant that wasn't the way it had actually worked.

"Problem number one," Riel said, "nobody saw anything. The guy who called it in, he lived right across from where it happened. He said he heard something, but what he heard didn't lead him to think that anything unusual had happened." I noticed he didn't tell me what exactly the guy said he had heard. I didn't ask. I didn't think I could stand knowing what it was. "He only called us because when he went to the door to let his cat in, he saw something lying in the street."

Something. He meant *someone.* Mom.

"When we did a canvass of the neighborhood later, a couple of other people said they had heard something, but nothing that had alarmed them. They also told us that they hadn't heard any car brakes squeal. They hadn't heard anything that you'd associate with a traffic accident. Nobody saw the car, let alone the driver. No one reported any cars speeding away in the area around the time it happened. None of the patrol cars in the area caught or even saw any speeders, either. So instead of starting out with a few useful leads, things that might have got us working on finding the person right away, we started with nothing."

I wanted to hear what he was saying, but at the same time I didn't want to hear it. I also wanted to know something: "Why are you telling me this?"

"Because I don't want you to think we did nothing." He leaned forward a little, like the closer he got to me, the better the chances were that I'd believe him. "It wasn't that we didn't care," he said. "It wasn't like that at all."

I still didn't get it. Why did it matter to him what I thought?

"We cared. We always care." He looked directly at me. "I'm sorry for how things turned out for you."

Sure. Whatever.

"Next step was the Ident guys," he said.

"Ident?"

"Forensic identification officers. The guys who come in and search the scene for evidence—you know, fingerprints, footprints, hair, and fibers. They document the crime scene and collect everything that might be useful. They checked for skid marks or tread marks that might show if the car had tried to stop suddenly or swerve out of the way—or if it hadn't. They didn't find any."

"What does that mean?"

Riel shrugged. "It could mean that whoever was

driving didn't see anyone on the street. Maybe the driver was impaired, you know, maybe they'd been drinking or taking drugs. Maybe the driver fell asleep at the wheel. Then the Ident officers started looking for anything that might help them identify the suspect car. There would have been quite an impact when a vehicle made contact, even if it was only going at the posted speed, which on your street is twenty-five miles per hour. The vehicle itself would have sustained some damage—a broken headlight, maybe—when it hit something."

That word again—*something*—when what he was talking about was my mother. Still, I guess he was trying to be nice, trying to spare my feelings by using some words instead of others.

"Sometimes it's the smallest things that can give us a clue. A piece of plastic from a headlight. Paint chips from the vehicle itself. Maybe the car drives through some mud that you can only find in a specific place and some of that mud gets transferred onto whatever the car hit. The Ident officers collected whatever they could and turned it all over to the forensic guys to see if they could help us narrow down the kind of car that was involved."

"But they couldn't, right?"

"Actually, they could. The chemistry section at the Centre of Forensic Sciences did a paint analysis. The way it works, the layers of paint on vehicles are often used on just a few models that were produced during a specific period of time. The manufacturers keep pretty good records and have samples of all the paints they use.

They make those available to the CFS. Plus, the CFS has its own reference collection of paints. They were able to tell us that the car was a General Motors Impala and the year it was manufactured. We knew what color it was, too. Hunter green. From that, we could check on all the cars registered in the area, then in the city, that were the same model, year, and color."

"And you didn't find anything, right?"

He sighed.

"We did a check on all the hunter green Impalas of the right age in the city—they were all accounted for, no damage, nothing. We put out an appeal to the public. We did a CrimeStoppers announcement asking anyone who had seen anything to come forward and tell us. Still nothing." He shook his head. "It's pretty rare to get absolutely no information. Sometimes someone who knows someone who owns a car that's the same make and model as a car that's been involved in a hit-and-run will contact us—maybe the person has been acting strangely. Or maybe a neighbor noticed something, or the guy's girlfriend or ex-girlfriend.

"Take your average citizen—maybe the guy's no saint, but he's got friends, family, people who care about him and interact with him and know when he's acting normal or when something's got him all antsy. Okay, so one night he does something stupid. He drinks too much or tokes up and, wham, he hits something on the road. Maybe he doesn't even know what it is at the time. But eventually he's going to find out. It was all over the news. And when he finds out, once he realizes what he's done and, for whatever reason, decides he's not going to go to the cops, he's going to start acting differently. Maybe he doesn't drive his car. Maybe he just keeps it in the garage. Maybe out of the blue he decides to get it painted. Maybe he starts drinking more than usual. There's always something that's going to tip off someone in that person's life that things aren't normal. You pair that up with the fact that his friends or family or whatever know what kind of car he's driving, and you'd expect someone to eventually say something. If you thought your friend Vin had been involved in something like that, you'd notice he was acting differently, right?"

I nodded. "Maybe I wouldn't run to the cops, though," I said. It sounded terrible, especially because we were talking about what had happened to my mother. But it was the truth.

"Maybe you wouldn't," Riel said. "Until you thought about it. Most people are all right, Mike. Most people want to do the right thing. But we got nothing. No one came forward. Best we could figure, maybe the car was stolen someplace else. A guy who stole a car would have a whole different group of friends—friends with maybe less incentive to come forward if a buddy did something wrong. So we checked Impalas that had been reported stolen. Did a pretty broad sweep, too. We didn't come up with any in the area, but we did pull one that had been reported stolen up in Simcoe the day before and was never recovered. After that . . ." His voice trailed off.

"You just gave up?"

"We hit a dead end. We don't quit when that happens. But other cases come up and they get assigned, and you have to try to clear those, too. Stuff happens. So even if you haven't closed that one, you can't give it one hundred percent of your attention."

"So that's it?"

He studied me with fog-gray eyes. He was so quiet for so long that I figured that really was it, that he had nothing else to say. Then he surprised me. "I never met your mother, Mike. But I have a pretty good idea what she was like."

Part of me wanted to tell him, No, you don't. You have no idea at all. But, I admit, I was curious.

"She worked hard," he said. "She always got to work on time and never left until she had everything done. She was always cheerful. The people she worked with liked her a lot. She took courses on her own time because she wanted to improve herself so she could get promoted. And while she was working hard, she was looking after you all by herself and looking after your uncle, too, until he was old enough to look after himself. She kept the house spotless—I saw that the first time I walked into the place. It's an old house, but you could tell by how everything sparkled that she was making the best home she could for her family. She liked to read, too, and she tried to get you reading, didn't she?"

My mother did love to read. She loved it more than watching TV. She used to read to me every night when

I was little. When I got older, she'd get me to cuddle up to her and she'd ask me to read to her.

"How did you know?"

"There were two stacks of library books on the coffee table in the living room. One was kids' books. The other was books for adults—fiction and nonfiction. She was well organized. She always returned her books on time, didn't she?"

That earned him another look of surprise from me. He smiled.

"She had the due date slips tacked to the bulletin board in the kitchen," he said. "She made sure you ate right—granola, not sugary cereals. Orange juice, not pop."

"I got pop on special occasions."

"She made her own jam." When I looked baffled, he said, "I saw it when your uncle opened the fridge to get milk for his coffee. Looked like homemade strawberry jam. She ever bake bread to go with it?"

"Yeah," I said, and my mouth watered just thinking about the smell from the oven. I looked at Riel with new interest. He was a lot smarter than I thought.

"It's not easy being a single mother," he said. "You have to work pretty hard just to pay the bills. It's pretty rough for some single parents—they're so busy trying to meet their financial obligations that they don't have enough time to make sure their kids turn out okay. From what I know about your mother, she was the kind of person who would have been determined to make sure that no matter what else happened, you went to school, did your homework, worked hard, and stayed out of trouble. Am I right?"

He was doing it again, trying to make me see myself through Mom's eyes. Only this time I didn't get mad at him.

He'd said he was sorry for how things had turned out for me. For all the stuff I'd lost, he meant. All the stuff that disappeared when Mom died.

"She wouldn't be too happy right now, would she, Mike?" he said. He stood up slowly. "You're in trouble right now, but you don't have to keep going in that direction. I just wanted to tell you that."

"I threw those cakes away," I said. I hadn't planned to say it. The words just popped out. Riel waited. "I didn't want to take them, but I did," I said. "Then I threw them away."

Riel didn't say anything. I don't know if he even believed me.

I sat there for a while after he left, then decided to go over to Vin's so that I could explain to him what had happened. Up near Danforth I spotted Jen. She wasn't alone. She was with a guy I had never seen before. She was holding his hand.

CHAPTER SEVEN

When you see your girlfriend holding hands with another guy, you've got a few options.

Option one: denial. Tell yourself you're not seeing what you're seeing. It's not what you think. Maybe she's landed the female lead in the school play and the guy whose hand she's holding is the male lead and they're rehearsing. Right out on the street where everyone can see them. But it doesn't *mean* anything. It's not real.

Option two: pretend you didn't see it. If you didn't see it, you don't have to deal with it. You can make believe she's still yours and yours alone, it's all cool.

Option three: deck the guy. What's he doing holding your girlfriend's hand? He must be pushing himself on her, because she's yours and she wouldn't hold some other guy's hand unless she was being forced to. And if some guy is forcing your girlfriend to do something she doesn't want to do, then the guy deserves whatever you feel like dishing out to him.

Option four: tell her it's over. If she's going to be holding someone else's hand, you don't want her holding yours anymore. After all, *she'd* play it that way, wouldn't she? If she saw you clinging to another girl, you'd be out of the picture so fast you'd start to doubt that you'd ever been in it.

Then there's what I did, which was wheel around and start walking as fast as I could in the opposite direction. And the whole time I was marching away, I kept hoping I'd hear her call, *Mike, Mike, stop, it's not what you think.*

It didn't happen.

» » »

Vin's mom answered the door. She's kind of tough looking. She's a waitress at a bar—has been forever. She wears a lot of makeup, even around the house, and she's got tons of hair, which she wears like one of Charlie's Angels on TV, only by now those angels are pretty middle-aged. Her voice is husky. Too many cigarettes and too much beer, Vin says. And she keeps strange hours—works until the bar closes at two in the morning, then comes home, does some housework, and sleeps until noon or so. She starts work at five thirty in the afternoon five days a week, Tuesday through Saturday. Which meant she was still home when I got to Vin's house. It was better than having to face Vin's dad, though. He works permanent evenings at a Ford plant.

Usually Vin's mom is nice to me. She kids us a lot, me and Vin and Sal. Calls us a posse. Tells us, "Don't do anything I wouldn't do," and then laughs because, according to Vin, there isn't a lot that his mom wouldn't do at least once. I guess grabbing boxes of cakes out of a bakery truck was one thing, though, because when she answered the door she didn't crack a smile, and when I asked if Vin was there, she stared at me for a moment before turning and calling him.

"Vincent!"

She never called Vin by that name unless she was good and mad at him. Vincent had been her father-in-law's name. Vin's mother never had anything good to say about Vin's grandfather. I don't even know why she agreed to name him after the old man.

While I was waiting for him—waiting to see if he'd even talk to me—she said, "What would your mother say?"

Jeez, it was that kind of day.

Vin slouched past his mom. She cuffed him on the butt. "You're not to leave this porch, do you understand me, Vincent?"

"Yeah."

He didn't even look at me. He walked to the porch railing, his back to me. I was sure he wasn't going to say a word. His mother went inside. When the door clicked shut behind her, Vin turned around.

"She wants to ground me for life." He sighed. "Still, it's better than my dad. He wants to kill me."

Vin's dad came across real tough. He was a nice guy, though. Every so often he'd come up with baseball tickets and he'd take all three of us to a game, me and Vin and Sal. He knew all the players on all the teams. Vin said the only part of the newspaper his dad ever read was the sports section, and the only magazine he ever opened was *Sports Illustrated.*

"I didn't tell them anything," I said.

"I know."

In a lousy day, one good thing had finally happened.

"I mean, I thought you had when I saw you at the door this morning and those two cops were coming up the walk right behind you. But then I thought about it, and I realized you'd never do that. You never ratted on me before."

"Riel says they probably asked around about who I hang out with," I told him. "He says it's basic police work."

He frowned. "How does he know that?"

"He used to be a cop."

This was news to Vin. "How do you know he wasn't the one who ratted me out? He's seen us together."

"I don't think so," I said. And, after a moment, "He investigated the hit-and-run." I didn't have to explain which hit-and-run.

"No kidding? So how come he's not a cop anymore?"

I realized I didn't know. The best I could do was shrug.

"Maybe because he was no good at it," Vin said. "Or maybe they fired him because he couldn't cut it. I mean, they never found out who killed your mom, right?"

I leaned against the porch railing and stared out at Vin's front lawn. It had more grass and fewer weeds than ours.

"He says they tried. He says no one saw anything."

"You talked to him about it?"

I told Vin how it had happened.

"And?" he said.

Good old Vin. We've known each other since day care. He did a lot of stupid stuff—like stealing boxes of cakes from a bakery truck—but he was my best friend. He knew me better than anyone, even better than Billy. He knew when something was bothering me.

"He says the car that hit her was probably stolen. He says whoever did it probably didn't see my mom because it doesn't look like they tried to brake or swerve. He says maybe whoever did it had been drinking or maybe they fell asleep at the wheel."

I could see Vin processing the information.

"And?" he said again.

"And I've been thinking," I said. "Would you get high if you were driving a stolen car? Would you take the chance you'd fall asleep at the wheel?"

He shrugged. "I've heard of stupider stuff," he said. "Besides, maybe he was a stupid car thief. Or a tired one."

"If I was driving around in a stolen car, I'd be a model citizen," I said. "I wouldn't want to attract any attention."

"If you were driving around in a stolen car, you'd be anything but a model citizen," Vin pointed out.

"A guy in a stolen car," I said. "Doesn't brake . . . Doesn't even swerve." It kept eating at me. "This is gonna sound crazy, but—" Could I say it out loud?

"You think whoever was driving *did* see her?" Vin said slowly. "He saw her, but didn't brake or swerve because . . . ?"

"You think it's possible?" I asked. "You think someone might have *wanted* to kill my mother on purpose?"

Vin's eyes met mine. They went all soft.

"Your mother was the greatest, Mike. Remember those chocolate chip cookies she used to make?" He smiled at the thought of them, and I could almost smell the warm chocolate. "And she never got mad at us, no matter what we did. You always got the feeling that she understood, you know what I mean?"

I knew exactly what he meant.

"Why would anyone want to kill her, Mike? What Riel said makes more sense, right?"

Didn't brake. Didn't swerve.

"Right, Mike?"

"Right," I said. But I kept thinking about it. How impaired did you have to be to not even see a person in the street right in front of you and to not even react? And if you were that impaired, then how could you vanish without a trace? *No one heard anything. No one saw anything. No one noticed a vehicle speeding in the area.* How could you be so messed up that you couldn't see where you were driving and what you were about to hit, then so on the ball that you managed to get away without a trace?

» » »

I thought it would be hard to find him, but it wasn't. He was right there in the phone book. Riel, John. The address listed was a house north of Danforth, a couple of blocks east of Greenwood. I was nervous as I approached it. There had only been one John Riel in the phone book and no J. Riels, so I figured it had to be him. But as I was going up the walk it occurred to me that maybe I was about to knock on the wrong door. I mean, he used to be a cop, right? Maybe cops kept their numbers unlisted, you know, for security reasons.

I started to turn back—call me a coward—when I saw someone coming around the side of the house, carrying a bag of groceries.

"Mike?" After Riel got over his surprise, he smiled. "What's up?"

"I need to ask you something."

"You had supper yet?"

I hadn't, but I lied and said I had.

"Well, I haven't," he said. "Come on in. If it's okay with you, we can talk while I cook."

I followed him up the steps and into the house. The place wasn't much bigger than my house, but it was a whole lot neater—a whole lot emptier, too. All the walls were painted white. There wasn't much furniture—a couch and a couple of chairs in the living room, a stereo set and a couple of well-stocked bookshelves, a table and chairs in the dining room, another smaller table and some chairs in the kitchen—and all of it was either black or chrome or both. The floors were bare—black and white tile in the front hall and the kitchen, hardwood everyplace else.

"Haven't lived here long, huh?" I said.

"A couple of years."

You could have fooled me. It looked like he had just moved in and hadn't got around to doing any decorating.

I followed him through to the kitchen.

"Have a seat," he said, waving to one of the black and chrome stools at the counter that divided the kitchen into a cooking area and an eating area. He started to unpack the bag of groceries—a couple of steaks, some potatoes, some lettuce, tomatoes, and a cucumber. Then he opened the fridge. "Soda?" he asked.

"Yeah, okay."

He pulled out a Coke for me and a beer for himself, opened them both, and shoved the Coke across the counter to me.

"You talk to Vin?"

I nodded.

"And it's all good?"

"Yeah."

Riel actually smiled.

"So, what can I do for you, Mike?"

It took a moment before I could get out the few words. "It's about my mom."

He pulled up a stool, sat across from me, and waited. He didn't say anything while I told him what I was thinking. He didn't say anything for a little while after I had finished, either. He just sipped his beer.

"So," he said finally, "what you're saying is maybe your mother was killed on purpose."

I nodded, grateful that he hadn't laughed.

"Do you know of any reason why anyone would want to do that, Mike?"

"Well, no," I had to admit.

He took another sip of beer.

"See, that's the thing about murder," he said. "In almost every case, the person who does it has a reason. He wants revenge. He's angry. The victim has something he wants badly. He's trying to stop someone from telling a secret. Stuff like that. What it means is, there's usually a link between the killer and the suspect—which is how we have a shot at solving cases. Pretty much we're successful, too. The ones we don't solve, and by that I mean, we don't make an arrest—" I wondered whether he noticed he was saying *we*, like he was still a cop. "In most of those cases, one of two things happens. One, we know who did it, but we can't prove it. We just can't get the evidence. Or, two, someone else knows who did it, but they won't tell. Gang killings are a good example. A lot of times a lot of people know who did it, but they won't tell because they're part of one of the gangs involved or they're citizens who are afraid of repercussions if they tell."

"What about serial killers?" I asked. "They don't usually know their victims."

"True," Riel said. He seemed kind of surprised, though. "But with serial killers, there's usually a pattern that helps you connect the dots. The killer picks the same general type of victim. He strikes in a particular geographic area or at a particular time of night or day. He uses a similar M.O. None of those things apply in the case of your mother. And I've got to tell you, Mike, I've never heard of a serial killer using an automobile as a murder weapon. That's not how they operate."

Okay, so maybe that was all true. But no matter how you looked at it, there was still one fact. "Someone was driving the car that killed my mother. Okay, so you have way more experience than me." A rookie cop first day on the job had more experience than me. "But I still don't see how someone could be so drunk or whatever that they couldn't see my mother in the street and then be so alert that they could get away without anyone seeing or hearing anything."

Riel took another sip of his beer and was quiet for a few more moments while he got up and scrubbed a couple of potatoes. He seemed to like to think things through before he answered. Then, finally, he said, "I hear what you're saying, Mike, but in the absence of any motive, there was no reason for us to think it was murder." He put the potatoes onto an aluminum pan and slid the pan into the oven. Then he stood with his back to me for a few moments while he washed the cucumber and the tomatoes. When he turned back to me, he said, "Suppose you tell me everything you remember from before it happened."

I frowned. "You mean, the day it happened?"

"The days before, the weeks before, whatever you can remember about what your mother might have done, where she might have gone, who she might have talked to, any arguments you remember her having with anyone, anything you can recall about her daily routine." He handed me the cucumber and the tomatoes. "And while you're at it, slice these nice and thin for me, will you?"

» » »

What did I remember? Everything, and nothing much at all. It had happened four years ago.

At quarter to eight every morning, five days a week, Monday to Friday, my mother left me with Mrs. McNab, a woman who lived across from my school. Mom had to be at work by eight-thirty, and school didn't start until a quarter to nine, so I spent an hour in Mrs. McNab's living room, quietly watching cartoons while Mr. McNab slept. After school I went back to Mrs. McNab's and had a snack—usually crackers and milk—until Mom came to pick me up again, which she usually did by about a quarter to six. Then we went home, and Mom made supper and I did my homework, and if there was any time, we read together.

On Fridays we went to Mr. Jhun's restaurant for supper. Mom did Mr. Jhun's books for him. Mr. and Mrs. Jhun really liked her. If Mrs. Jhun wasn't too busy—and even if she was—she would come and sit with us for a while and talk to Mom. That ended about a month before Mom died, though, when Mr. Jhun was killed.

Riel perked up when I mentioned Mr. Jhun.

"The Korean guy, right?"

I nodded.

"You knew him?"

"Sure," I said. I told him that we always sat at the booth closest to the cash register—that was our spot on Friday night. If we were ever late coming in, there was always a little reserved sign sitting on the table. From there, Mom could chitchat with Mrs. Jhun, who ran the cash register whenever the place was busy, and it was always busy on Friday night. Because we sat close to the cash register, Mom and I noticed one night that Mr. and Mrs. Jhun seemed to be having some kind of disagreement. In Korean, of course. This was unusual. Most times they got along pretty well. But one night there was no mistaking the fact that Mrs. Jhun was upset about something and that Mr. Jhun wasn't agreeing with whatever she was saying. After a while Mrs. Jhun came over and sat in the booth next to Mom. Mom took one look at her and sent me over to the counter. She knew I loved to spin around and around on the stools and, for once, she didn't object. The two of them talked for a long time, until I had spun around so many times that I thought I was going to throw up. On the way home, I asked Mom what Mrs. Jhun had been so upset about. She wouldn't tell me—she said it was none of my business—but later that night, when Billy came over, I heard Mom telling Billy about it. The fact that she was even talking to Billy about Mr. Jhun told me something. She knew Billy didn't care about the old man. She'd got mad at Billy a couple of times because he had made jokes about foreigners, especially the Chinese, even though Mr. Jhun wasn't even Chinese.

"It's bad enough he keeps that gold coin right on top of the cash register where anyone could walk away with it," Mom said. Mr. Jhun's gold coin sat in a little glass case. He called it his good luck charm. Sometimes he used to let me play with it. It was smooth and cool and heavy in my hand. "But the main thing is, he has far too much cash around," Mom went on. "It should be in a bank, but he doesn't like banks. She tries to reason with him. So do I. I tell him that I keep all my money in the bank." I heard a little laugh and could imagine what was going through her mind—*all* my money, like she was loaded. "She's so upset, and I don't know what to do about it. She said she had a bad-luck feeling about the restaurant. The place that was there before burned down. You remember, Billy, almost the whole block went up in flames five or six years ago. And apparently the man who owned the place before that had a heart attack and died in the walk-in freezer."

"Yeah, that's bad luck, all right," Billy had said. He sounded like he was only half-listening to what Mom was saying.

"It's not that this is a bad neighborhood. It isn't. But

it's just not smart to keep so much cash lying around."

"How much money are we talking about?" Billy asked. It was his favorite question, along with, "How much do you think that cost?"

"A lot," Mom said. "More than I'd know what to do with."

"From that dump?" Billy said. "A lot of people around here must have bad taste."

"He does everything in cash," Mom says. "Pays all his suppliers cash. And he runs that catering business on the side. You'd be surprised how well a person can do when he works hard, Billy."

It was a gentle dig. From where I was sitting on the stairs, I could hear Mom sigh. "Now Mrs. Jhun has me all worried. Maybe I should have a talk with him. Maybe I should take him down to my bank and introduce him to the manager."

Billy laughed. "You're Mike's mom. You're always acting like you're my mom. That's enough, don't you think? This Mr. John—"

"Jhun," my mother corrected.

"Whatever," Billy said. "I'm sure he can look after himself."

Billy turned out to be wrong. Mr. Jhun's restaurant was robbed less than a week later. The restaurant had been closed at the time, and the Jhuns were in their upstairs apartment. Mr. Jhun had gone downstairs, where he had surprised a robber and got himself killed in the process.

"A couple of weeks later, Mom went to say good-bye to Mrs. Jhun," I told Riel, "and she ended up getting run over." My throat got tight and I felt my eyes sting the way they always did when I thought about that night. "I don't know, maybe Mrs. Jhun was right, maybe it was all just part of the place's bad luck."

Riel had been raising his bottle of beer to his lips, but he stopped all of a sudden and looked at me.

"Excuse me?" he said.

"Bad luck," I said. "Not that Mrs. Jhun is superstitious or anything. She isn't one of those people who throws salt over their shoulders or freaks out every time she sees a black cat. But she gets these feelings sometimes."

"Are you sure your mother went to see Mrs. Jhun the night she died?"

I nodded.

Riel closed his eyes for a moment. When he opened them again, he was shaking his head.

"We asked around," he said. "We asked everyone in the area, everyone who knew your mother. We talked to your uncle. I'm pretty sure we even had someone talk to you."

A face flashed into my memory. A woman in a police uniform. She asked me a lot of questions about my mother and handed me a tissue when I started to cry.

"She was out doing errands," Riel said. "That's what your uncle told us. So did his girlfriend, what was her name?"

"Kathy," I said.

"Yeah. That's what she said Billy had told her. We know she went to Shoppers Drug Mart—she had a bag with her—a tube of toothpaste, a container of laundry detergent, and a Simpsons comic book."

Jeez, the guy had a photographic memory. Either that, or he had been peeking in some files recently.

"We know from the cash register tape that she was there about forty-five minutes before she . . ." He skipped the next word. "It's about a twenty-minute walk from the store to your house," he said slowly. "We asked, but we couldn't find anyone who could help us account for the missing time. And nobody said anything about her being at that restaurant." His eyes were sharp on me. "Why didn't you tell us?"

"I thought you knew," I said. "I mean, isn't that your job? And, anyway, I didn't know where she was until after Mrs. Jhun came back."

"Came back? You're losing me, Mike."

"Right after Mr. Jhun died and the police weren't making any progress in finding who killed him, Mrs. Jhun started to get sick. So her sister insisted she go back to Korea where she could look after her. The night my mother died, she saw Mrs. Jhun at the restaurant. The place was closed up. Mrs. Jhun was saying good-bye. She got into a taxi and went to the airport. She didn't even know my mother was dead until she came back to Canada about nine months ago."

Riel ducked into the fridge and pulled out some green onions.

"Cut these up, too, would you?" he said. "Nice thin pieces." When I was finished, he said. "Where can I find Mrs. Jhun?"

There was a bite to his voice, and it crossed my mind that maybe he thought she'd had something to do with it.

"She was Mom's friend," I said.

"I just want to make sure someone talks to her, Mike, that's all." He was looking directly at me and talking in a calm, quiet voice so I couldn't do anything but believe him, even though I wasn't sure I should. I told him Mrs. Jhun's address. He pulled a steak out of the fridge and looked at me. "You sure you're not hungry?"

I was practically drooling at the thought of steak, but I said no. "I ate already."

He peered at me some more before nodding. "I'm going to take a look into this," he said, "talk to a few of my friends. But I'm not making any promises. We looked at this thing every which way when it happened. Okay?"

I said okay. Then I held my breath all the way home, hoping. Just hoping, that's all.

CHAPTER EIGHT

I flung open the screen door so hard that it clattered against the brick. I burst into the house, feeling like my heart was going to explode in my chest.

"Jeez," Billy said. He appeared so suddenly in the doorway to the living room that I almost collided with him. "I thought we'd been hit by a tornado or something. Where have you been, anyway?"

"The cops are going to reopen Mom's case," I told him. "Riel is going to talk to them about it, get them to take another look at what happened."

"Yeah?" Billy didn't sound nearly as excited as I was. But then, the main things that excited him were a night out with his friends, a night in with his girlfriend, or the chance to make some easy money. "How did that happen?"

"I was talking to him. I told him about Mrs. Jhun. It turns out he didn't know about that. So he said he'd look into it."

"What about Mrs. Jhun?"

"She saw Mom the night she died."

I had the weird feeling that I was speaking a language Billy didn't understand. He was staring at me, but he didn't seem to be registering anything I was saying.

"What are you talking about, Mikey?" he said.

"I thought they knew. I didn't know myself until a little while ago, but I thought they must have known because they're the cops, right? They're supposed to know stuff, that's their job."

"Slow down, sport," Billy said. He took a step closer to me. "What's all this about Mrs. John?"

"Maybe it's nothing, but Riel told me the cops ran out of leads and that part of the reason for that was that they couldn't find anyone who remembered seeing Mom that night. They know she went to the drugstore, but that's all they know. But she saw Mrs. Jhun at the restaurant."

"The restaurant was closed then, Mike," Billy said. "It closed right after the old Chinese guy was killed, remember? They closed it down and never opened it up again."

"I know. And Mrs. Jhun decided to go back to Korea to stay with her sister. She left that night. Mom dropped by her place to say good-bye to her. Then Mrs. Jhun took a taxi to the airport. She never even knew Mom had that accident. Or that the police were trying to find people who had seen Mom that night. By the time Mrs. Jhun came back here, the cops had given up on the case, and I didn't even think about it until I was talking to Riel and—"

Billy put his hands on my shoulders and sort of squeezed me.

"Hey, calm down, Mikey," he said. "You're getting pretty worked up over what will probably turn out to be nothing."

"But Riel said he'd look into it. He said—"

"Looking into something isn't the same as doing anything about it," Billy said. His face was all mashed up, like it was painful for him to have to say the words. "Jeez, it was a hit-and-run over four years ago now. They never found the car that did it. They never found the driver. I know you want to know what happened to your mom, Mike. I do, too. She was my sister. She practically raised me. But if it's been four years and they haven't found out who did it, what do you think their chances are now? Whoever did it probably got rid of the car years ago."

"But the cops are solving all kinds of old cases these days," I said. I didn't want someone to tell me what couldn't happen. I wanted someone to tell me what *had* happened.

"I read the papers sometimes, too," Billy said. "The cases they're solving are cases that involve DNA, cases where they have some leads. This isn't that kind of case, Mike."

By now my mood was as flat as a stale Coke. Maybe Billy was right. After all, if Mrs. Jhun had noticed anything unusual or important, wouldn't she have said so by now? She had seen Mom. I knew because she had told me. Mom had stopped by Mrs. Jhun's place and had wished her a safe journey. Then Mrs. Jhun had gotten into a taxi, and the last thing she remembered was seeing my mother walking down Danforth toward home.

"You got homework?" Billy said.

Jeez, where did that question come from?

"You're in trouble, remember?" Billy said. "You let your schoolwork slide anymore and it's not going to look good when you have to show up in court and try to convince some judge that you're an okay kid who just made one mistake."

"You feeling all right, Billy?" I asked, kind of joking.

"Do your homework, Mike."

I headed for the living room, thinking I'd sprawl on the couch to get my work done, same as I always did. Billy blocked my path.

"We've got company," he said.

I peeked into the room. It was Dan and Lew, each with a beer in his hand. Dan saluted me with his beer bottle.

"Here's to homework and high school," he said. "The best thing you can say about either is, when they're over, they're over for good."

"Amen to that," Lew said.

"Two more years, Mike," Dan said, "and you'll be a free man, just like us."

Two more years. Seven hundred and thirty days. As

good as a lifetime away. I sighed and went upstairs to my room to do my homework.

» » »

Friday got off to a bad start. I woke up with a headache that only got worse as I stood on the corner of Jen's street. I had been planted there for so long that I thought maybe I'd missed her. Only how could that be? I had arrived extra early. There's no way she could have got by me, unless she had all of a sudden decided to go to school at six in the morning. I was about to give up—I didn't need any late notices—when I saw her come out of her driveway carrying a big box. She started down the sidewalk toward me, moving fast, like she knew she was late, then skidded to a stop when she saw me. She glanced back over her shoulder—she was checking to see if her mother was standing at a door or a window.

I stayed put. Rushing up to her would have been a big mistake when she was worried about what her mother was or wasn't seeing. Instead, I waited for her to come to me.

"Hi," she said. She glanced at me, but just barely, like she didn't care about me anymore. Like maybe she cared about someone else instead, maybe a tall blond by the name of Patrick.

I wrestled the box out of her arms. I wanted to score some points by carrying it for her.

"It's okay, I can manage," she said.

"Hey, no problem," I said. I smiled at her. She didn't

smile back. “What is it, anyway?”

“It’s a cake,” she said. “The Girls’ Athletic Association is having a bake sale to raise money for uniforms.”

“Bet it’ll sell out in no time,” I said. Then, because she wasn’t talking and I didn’t know what to say, I said, “Vin and Sal got busted, too.”

“I heard.”

Oh.

“I also heard that the police asked you who was with you and you refused to tell them.”

“Yeah.”

Those green eyes turned on me. “Why didn’t you tell them?”

“What?” I couldn’t believe she was asking. “You mean, why didn’t I rat out my friends?”

“It was their fault, wasn’t it?” Jen said. “I know you, Mike. I know you wouldn’t do something like that if Vin wasn’t pushing you. He’s a petty criminal. You’re not like that.”

“Whoa, wait a minute. What are you talking about? Vin’s my best friend.”

“Everyone says it was his idea. Isn’t that right?”

Yeah, it was right. But how would it look if I blamed it all on Vin? I mean, I caught the box he threw to me. I ran after him and Sal. I even ate some pie.

“We all decided together,” I said. It wasn’t true, but it means something when a guy’s your best friend.

Her mouth tightened. She looked so much like her mother that it was scary.

"You're telling me that it was your idea to steal from that truck?" she said.

"It was just a couple of boxes of cake."

"It's a crime. You could end up in big trouble."

"I'm a minor," I reminded her. Another mistake.

"So you think you can just do whatever you want, is that it? You think nothing's going to happen to you?"

Jeez, what was going on?

"Jen, what I did was wrong. I admit it. I got caught."

"And you refused to cooperate with the police."

"They're my friends!" Why couldn't she understand that? "I'm going to court. I'm going to pay for what I did. And it's not like I'm planning to do it again."

"I defended you," she said.

"What?"

"To my parents. I defended you. *Both* times."

"What do you mean, both times?" But I already knew. "I never touched your dad's bike."

Sweet Jen. She didn't look so sweet now.

"You were in the house just before the bike was stolen," she said. "You saw where we keep our keys."

Jen's parents had a key rack in the shape of a big key hanging in the kitchen.

"I never touched your dad's bike," I said again. "This is about that guy, right?"

"What guy?"

"That son of your mother's friend, what's his name?"

"What does Patrick have to do with this?"

Five. Four. Three. Two. One.

"Are you going out with him or what, Jen?"

Her cheeks turned crimson. Jen couldn't lie to me even if she wanted to, not with her instant blush. I'll give her credit, though. She didn't even try. Her eyes filled with tears.

"Great!" I said. Then, stupid, stupid, stupid, I lifted the box and threw it down to the sidewalk. Jen let out a cry. The box crumpled, which probably wasn't good news for the cake inside. I was too mad to care. I turned and marched to school. I don't know and didn't care what Jen did.

» » »

I don't know what I thought would happen, but I thought something would. I sat in history class, trying to ignore my pounding head and the queasy feeling in my stomach. I kept checking Riel's expression, sure I'd see some hint in the way he looked at me, or that he'd call me over after class to give me some big news. But I didn't see anything, and he didn't call me over. At the end of class I started up to his desk to ask him what was going on, but Vin grabbed me before I got halfway there.

"Party tonight?" he said.

I turned to him automatically, then swung around to find Riel. He was gone.

"Huh?" I said.

"Party tonight?"

"Aren't you grounded, Vin?" The way he had told

it, he'd be lucky to get out of the house again before he turned twenty-one.

"What's grounded mean when your parents aren't around to enforce it?" he said. "That's like getting spanked by a guy with no hands. My cousin Frank is having some people over. Melinda's going to be there." He must have read the lack of recognition in my eyes. "That girl I was telling you about. Jeez, do you ever listen to me? Come on. You've got to meet her. Maybe she has a friend."

I shrugged. Why not? I had nothing better planned. The way things were going, I had nothing planned for the rest of my life.

I almost backed out at the last minute. My headache faded, but my stomach started to feel jumpy.

"It's stress," Vin said, like all of a sudden he had a medical degree. "You've got to meet this girl. You've just got to."

So I went to the party with Vin. Sal wanted to come, but he was grounded, too, and his dad was home to enforce the punishment. Melinda was there, and Vin was right about her being gorgeous. As for having feelings for Vin, though, well, if you count the way a girl feels when she rolls her eyes every time a guy asks her to dance, then, yeah, I guess she had feelings. Which almost made me laugh, because if you looked at it in the right light, Jen had feelings for me too.

Melinda's friends were all there with guys, which left Vin and me pretty much out in the cold—not that this prevented Vin from trying to catch her attention. I hung around the food table, eating chips and dip, drinking Coke, trying to look like I was into the music and didn't care that no one was paying attention to me. Then, like a volcano erupting, it happened. I tried to get to the bathroom, but I didn't make it.

"Eeew!" said one girl. Melinda, I think.

"Jeez," Vin said. "I've never seen anyone puke up that much stuff."

Vin's cousin Frank got mad.

I felt dizzy. I threw up again. Then, I'm not sure how, Billy showed up with Dan and Lew. Billy shoveled me into the back seat of his Toyota. We'd only gone a few miles when I felt like more stuff was about to come up. Billy hit the brakes and hauled me out headfirst onto the side of the road.

"You're gonna puke, fine," a voice said. Billy sounded ticked off. "But you're not gonna puke in my car, Mikey. No way."

Someone laughed, but I didn't have time to see whether it was Dan or Lew. I was too busy throwing up.

"You done?" Billy said after a few minutes. His nose wrinkled in disgust, but his hands were gentle as he guided me back to the car. "There's some mouthwash in the glove compartment," he said to Dan. Billy was always interested in being fresh for a girl. "Hand it to me, will you?"

Dan handed out the bottle. Billy unscrewed the cap and shoved it at me. "Rinse and spit," he said. "You'll feel better."

I did. Then he opened the car door and helped me get back in.

"You got a lot to learn, Mikey," Dan said. "When he was your age, Billy could do a twelve-pack, no problem."

"I wasn't drinking," I said. I don't even like the taste of beer. "I don't feel so good."

"Mike's a good kid," Billy said. "The white sheep of the family." Usually when he said that, he was teasing me. But he didn't sound like he was teasing tonight. Tonight he sounded more like he was defending me.

"If you don't count robbing a bakery truck," Dan said with a shrug. "Or that bike thing."

He laughed, then he and Billy got in the front. I got in the back again with Lew.

The car lurched forward. So did my stomach. I had to fight to keep from spewing again.

"You feel like you're gonna be sick again, you let me know, right, Mikey?"

"I want to go home."

"Not gonna happen, Mike. Not yet, anyway. I got plans of my own. You just close your eyes and try to sleep. You just got a little bug, but you're gonna be fine."

When I closed my eyes, my head started to throb. Then the car started to spin. Finally the whole world was revolving around me, like I was the sun and the universe was wheeling out of control. I scrabbled for the window, got it down, and hung my head out.

"Jeez," Billy groaned, slowing the car to a stop again. "Mikey, you're barfing all over the side of my vehicle."

"Could be worse," Dan said. "He could be ruining a decent paint job instead of that home-done patch job of yours."

"Courtesy of the Rembrandt of automobiles, I suppose," Billy said.

"Quality workmanship," Dan said, "even if I do say so myself."

"And you do," Lew said. "All the time."

» » »

I must have fallen asleep, like Billy said I would, because the next thing I remembered was waking up in the backseat with sun streaming in through the streaky window. Someone had thrown a blanket over me. I was the only person in the car, which was parked in an alley somewhere I didn't recognize. I sat up slowly. My head didn't ache anymore, but my stomach still felt rocky. My tongue felt like a big wet sock, but the inside of my mouth was as dry as old paint. I would have traded Billy's car for a bottle of water.

I sat up for a few moments, and when that didn't make me feel any worse, I edged the car door open and slid out. Where was I, anyway?

The alley ran for a couple of blocks in either direction. The buildings that backed onto it were all low-rises, none of them more than three or four stories high. I didn't recognize any of them, not from the back, anyway. And I had no idea where Billy was. So I did the only thing I could think of—I circled around to the driver's door, opened it, leaned in, and honked the horn a couple of times.

Nothing.

I tried again. This time I heard someone swear. A door opened, and Billy's head poked out. He was fully dressed, but I knew from the look on his face and the way his hair was sticking out in a hundred different directions that I had just woken him.

"I want to go home," I said.

"So, jeez, go then. You don't have to wake up the whole neighborhood."

"I don't have any money, Billy. I don't know where we are. And I don't feel good."

"You can be such a pain," he said. Then, there it was, that crazy old Billy smile. He pressed a palm against my forehead. For a flash, he reminded me of Mom. "You're not hot," he said. "I guess that's good." He glanced back at the door he had just come out of and sighed. "I was out here maybe five or six times last night," he said, "checking on you. I wanted to bring you inside, but Dan didn't want you barfing and ruining the party."

"Where are we, anyway?"

"Dan and Lew's place." When I looked lost, he added, "Their *new* place. They moved in a few months ago."

As I got into the car, I peered at the building. "What is it, a house?"

"It's a garage, Einstein," Billy said. "A garage with an apartment on top. Dan owns the garage—does wicked paint jobs on his own now. He and Lew live in the apartment. What a setup. Someday I'm going to have a place like that."

Billy drove me home. After he let me out, he sat in the car for a minute. Then he swore under his breath, got out, and slammed the door.

"I'm too tired to drive all the way back there." He punched me, but not hard. "Next time you don't feel so good, don't go out, okay, Mike? I got things to do. I can't be picking you up from parties all the time."

All the time. Like he had ever picked me up from a party before.

I followed him into the house. He went straight upstairs. I heard two thumps—his boots hitting the floor—then a thud—his body hitting the mattress. I went into the kitchen and fumbled in the little corner cabinet where Mom used to keep her spices. Most of them were gone now or dried out and tasteless. Up on the top shelf was a plastic bottle of acetaminophen. I shook out a couple of tablets and swallowed them down with a couple of tumblers of water. Then I went into the living room and sprawled on the couch.

By noon my headache was gone and my stomach no longer felt like it would explode any minute. I lay on the couch, still feeling a little queasy, when suddenly my brain clicked into gear. Riel had promised to look into things. He had said he would talk to some of his friends. Did that mean someone was going to talk to Mrs. Jhun? Had they talked to her already? I showered, changed my clothes, drank another glass of water, and headed over to her house.

» » »

She was sitting on her porch, a sweater over her shoulders, a teacup in her hand. She didn't look at me, even when I was climbing the steps right in front of her.

"Mrs. Jhun?"

She stared straight ahead.

"Are you okay, Mrs. Jhun?"

She turned and studied me a moment, and I got the feeling that she wasn't wondering *who* I was so much as *what* I was.

"Michael," she said at last. "Please, come and sit down."

I pulled up a chair beside her.

"Are you sure you're okay, Mrs. Jhun?"

"What can I do for you, Michael?"

"I was wondering if the police had been here to speak to you."

"The police? Why would the police want to speak to me?"

That answered that question. They hadn't visited her yet, which meant that either Riel hadn't got around to talking to his friends, or his friends hadn't got around to talking to Mrs. Jhun.

"It's about the night Mom died. You saw her that night, remember? You told me about it."

Mrs. Jhun nodded.

"She came to say good-bye." A lopsided smile sat on her lips. Her eyes seemed to be focused on something far in the distance. I wondered if she was seeing something I wasn't, or if she was just remembering.

"You were leaving the restaurant for the last time," I said, "and Mom came by and you spoke to her, right?"

She nodded again. Slowly up, slowly down, as if her head weighed a hundred pounds. I realized I wasn't the only one who didn't feel well.

"Do you remember anything else about that night?" I asked. "Did you see anyone on the street? Did you see Mom talk to anyone or notice anyone following her?"

"She bought a comic book for you," she said. "She showed it to me."

"That's right!" Great, she remembered. She remembered details from that night. "What else, Mrs. Jhun? What else do you remember?"

"She told me she was going to miss me," she said. "I think she is the only person who told me that. *I will miss you.*" Mrs. Jhun whispered the words. "She hugged me before I got in the taxi. Your mother always hugged people."

She used to hug me maybe a dozen times a day. By the time I was eleven, I was squirming away from her as soon as I saw her coming toward me, arms outstretched. "Aw, Mom!" I'd say. "Jeez, I'm almost twelve!" Like that made me too old for all that stuff. Now I would have killed for one of those hugs.

"She hugged me and I got into the taxi and she walked away. She was going home to give you the comic book after you brushed your teeth. She said you never liked to brush your teeth."

That was true. But a couple of years ago the dentist found some cavities. That cured me of toothbrush avoidance. If you ask me, five minutes at the sink beats five seconds under a dentist's drill any day of the week, not to mention all the squawking Billy did when he had to pay the bill.

"She stopped and talked to that man, too," she said. "She was friendly to everyone."

"What man?"

Mrs. Jhun smiled. "The man with the shiny mouth," she said. "He sparkled like the sun."

"The man with the shiny mouth?"

She closed her eyes and leaned back in her chair.

"Mrs. Jhun, are you okay?"

"This has been a long day, Michael," she said. It was only two o'clock in the afternoon. "I am very tired." She started to get up but was unsteady on her feet. She gripped the arm of the aluminum chair she had been sitting on. The chair wobbled. I jumped up and grabbed her arm to support her. She leaned on me all the way to the door.

"Goodnight, Michael," she said as she slipped inside.

Goodnight?

"Mrs. Jhun—"

The door closed softly in my face. I stood on the

porch, trying to decide what to do. Confused, I retreated down the steps. When I reached the sidewalk I looked back at Mrs. Jhun's house. Then I went looking for a different kind of answer.

CHAPTER NINE

I didn't hesitate on Riel's front walk this time. I marched straight onto his porch and hammered on the door. When Riel appeared, he had a tenth grade history textbook in one hand and a notebook in the other.

"There's a doorbell, you know," he said. "Saves wear and tear on the door."

"You said you were going to talk to your friends. You said you were going to look into what happened."

"You want to come inside, Mike?"

"No! I want to know why you lied to me."

He stepped aside quietly and waited until I forgot that I had said I didn't want to come in.

"You thirsty?" he asked.

"Nobody's talked to her yet."

He stuck a pen in the textbook to mark his place, then set the book on the table next to the telephone.

"Mrs. Jhun, you mean?" he said. At least he had

remembered her name. I nodded. "Excuse me," he said. He picked up the phone and punched in some numbers. "Steve? Riel. Look, about that favor I asked you?" He glanced at me while he listened to whatever Steve was saying. "Yeah, sure," he said at last. "You let me know."

He sighed as he set the receiver back into the cradle. It didn't sound like a good omen.

"I used to work with Steve," he said. "He's a good cop."

"He didn't talk to her, did he?"

"Not yet."

"But he's going to?"

"He's going to see what he can do."

Jeez! "What does that mean?"

"It means that he's a busy guy. I don't know whether you're aware of it or not, but the police service is laboring under severe budget constraints. Used to be someone grabbed your wallet, a cop would show up at your house inside of thirty minutes to take your information. It's not like that anymore, Mike."

"You're comparing my mom's death to a stolen wallet?"

"No, I'm not." He didn't raise his voice to match mine, didn't seem annoyed that I was yelling at him. "But we're talking about something that happened a few years ago, and these guys are up to their eyeballs in stuff that happened this week, if not this morning. He says he's going to get to it. And if says he will, he will. I know this guy, Mike."

I believed him. I didn't want to. I didn't think I'd ever want to believe something a cop—well, an ex-cop—

told me. But with Riel, I just did. I can't explain it. He reached for his textbook and started to open it.

"She remembers something," I said.

The book stayed closed.

"You talked to her?"

"I went over to ask her if the police had been around. She told me she saw Mom talking to some guy with a shiny mouth."

"A shiny mouth? What do you mean?"

"I don't know," I admitted. "I'm not even sure she knows what she meant. She was acting kind of strange. I don't think she's feeling well."

"What do you mean?"

I told him about how she hadn't noticed me at first, and about her lopsided smile and the funny expression on her face. I told him how unsteady she had been on her feet, and how tired she was.

When I said she had told me "Good-night," Riel said, "I hope she doesn't live alone."

"She does," I said. "Why?"

"Is she generally in good health?"

I said I didn't know.

"How old would you say Mrs. Jhun is, Mike?"

I didn't know that, either.

"But you know where she lives, right?"

"Yeah."

"Come on. Show me."

We drove to Mrs. Jhun's house. Riel did a sloppy job of parking in front of it. I would have thought a cop could drive better than that, but I guessed they could park pretty much where they wanted to, so maybe careful parking wasn't a top priority for them. Riel bounded up the steps and hammered on the door.

"There's a doorbell." I pointed to it before I pressed it. "Saves wear and tear on the door."

He pressed on the bell, waited, and pressed again.

"Maybe she went out," I said.

"Maybe." He crossed the porch and, shading his eyes, peered into the window. Suddenly he was back at the door, trying the knob with one hand and pulling a cell phone out of his pocket with the other.

"What's the matter?"

He tossed the phone to me. "Dial 911. Give them the address. Tell them there's someone unconscious inside, you don't know the cause. Tell them to send an ambulance."

"What's wrong? What's—"

"Just do it, Mike," he said.

He stepped back a pace and went at the door foot-first. He had to kick it twice before he got it open, and by then I had a 911 dispatcher on the line. My voice was shaking as I gave her the information. I hung up and went inside.

Mrs. Jhun was lying on the living room floor. The teacup she had been carrying the last time I saw her lay shattered nearby. Riel was bending over her.

"She's breathing," he said, and he sounded relieved, which scared me. It hadn't occurred to me that she might not be. "Hand me that blanket."

I grabbed the knitted blanket that Mrs. Jhun had draped over the back of her couch. Riel laid it over her, covering her up to her chin.

"You get through to 911?" he asked.

I nodded. "They're sending someone." I looked at Mrs. Jhun. I always used to tease her that she looked so young, but she didn't look young anymore. She looked old and frail, and it started to seem possible that she was dying.

"Sit down, Mike," Riel said.

I heard the words, but couldn't make myself act on them. I kept staring at Mrs. Jhun lying there, looking so helpless.

"Mike!"

I looked from Mrs. Jhun to Riel.

"Sit down, Mike, before you fall down." Again with the calm voice, the one that made you think he had the situation under control, even if he didn't. I backed over to the couch and dropped down onto it.

Pretty soon I heard the bleating of an ambulance siren. Car doors opened and slammed. Footsteps thundered on the porch steps, then on the porch, and then the room filled with paramedics and equipment and a gurney. Riel calmly filled them in, then stepped back. He nodded to me.

"Come on."

"I want to see what's happening."

He touched my arm. "Let's wait outside, Mike, and let the professionals do their job."

I didn't want to leave, but I got up anyway, and we went outside. By now, any neighbors that were around had come out of their houses and were either standing on their porches or down on the sidewalk, wanting to know what had happened.

"You think she's going to be okay?" I asked.

"I don't know," Riel said. At least it was an honest answer.

The paramedics came out of the house with Mrs. Jhun on the gurney. Her eyes were still closed. Riel followed them to the ambulance. I saw him asking questions as they loaded her inside. My heart almost stopped when they slammed the ambulance door. Riel came back onto the porch.

"They're taking her to East General," he said. "You want to go?"

I nodded and headed for the car. He tossed me his keys.

"I'll be right there," he said.

I wanted to tell him, "Now! I want to go now!" Then I saw what he was doing. He went over to the small group of people who were standing on the sidewalk and started talking to them. I don't know what he asked, but one of the people stepped forward. I recognized her. She lived next door to Mrs. Jhun. Sometimes they had tea together. Riel talked to her, gesturing back toward the house. He took a notebook out of his pocket, wrote down something, then tore out the sheet and handed it to the woman. Finally he came back to the car.

"The next-door neighbor is going to call someone

to fix the door," he said as he turned the key in the ignition. "She says most of the family is back in Korea but that there's a niece in Vancouver. You know their names or how to get in touch with them?"

I didn't. "But they write to her all the time," I said, "and I know she telephones them on Sundays. She always waits until the rates are low."

Riel nodded. "I'll drop you at the hospital, then come back and see if I can find their phone numbers."

The East General emergency room was packed, but it didn't take long for Riel to find out that Mrs. Jhun was there and being seen by a doctor.

"This could take a while," he warned me.

I didn't care. I didn't have anything better to do.

"I'll be back as soon as I can," Riel promised.

He was back thirty minutes later. He went straight to the nurse on duty, and I saw him give her a piece of paper. He talked to her for a while. When he came and claimed the chair next to mine in the waiting room he said, "Apparently she's had a stroke."

"Is that bad?"

"It can be really bad," he said, which surprised me. A lot of grown-ups would have just told me not to worry.

We waited through three cups of coffee for Riel and two cans of Coke for me and still nothing happened. Riel asked me if I wanted something to eat. My stomach had settled down a lot, but I wasn't interested in food.

"I'm not hungry," I said.

He didn't push the issue.

Then I saw a woman with a stethoscope slung around her neck talking to the same nurse Riel had spoken to. When the nurse pointed out Riel, the woman looked faintly surprised. She came toward us. I nudged Riel and we both got to our feet.

"John?" she said. There were little frown marks between her eyes.

"Susan." Riel turned to me. "Mike, this is Dr. Thomas."

"You know Mrs. John?" Dr. Thomas asked Riel.

"Jhun," I said. "It's Jhun."

Riel introduced me and said, "She's a family friend of Mike's. We found her."

"Do you know how to contact her family?"

"I gave the information to the nurse," Riel said.

"How is she?" I asked.

Dr. Thomas glanced at Riel before saying, "Her condition is grave. We'll contact her family, John, but . . ." She shrugged.

"Can I see her?" I asked.

"Not right now, Mike," Dr. Thomas said. "Maybe in a while."

Maybe. Not definitely.

It was late in the day by now. "I'm going to take Mike home," Riel said. "You've got my cell number. Call me if anything happens, Susan, okay?"

She said she would.

» » »

Riel drove me home—it wasn't far—but I couldn't make myself get out of the car, not without knowing for sure.

"Grave, that's not good, is it?" I said. That's how Dr. Thomas has described Mrs. Jhun's condition. Grave.

Riel looked straight at me and shook his head. "It's about as bad as it gets," he said. Jeez, the guy never sugar-coated anything. "But it doesn't mean the situation can't turn around."

"You think it will?"

I couldn't read what was in the long, hard look he gave me.

"I'm not a doctor, Mike. I really don't know." It was quiet in the car again. It seemed like it was quiet in the whole world. Then, "You had anything to eat today?"

I shook my head. For the first part of the day, food was about the last thing I wanted to think about. After that, everything else had crowded out the idea.

Riel turned the key in the ignition. "I don't think too well on an empty stomach," he said.

We ended up at a tiny restaurant down on Queen Street near Coxwell. I guessed it wasn't much of a coincidence that there was a cop shop right up the street. Riel claimed the booth in the very back and flagged the waitress over.

"They do great ribs here, Mike," he said. "You like ribs?"

The last time I had had ribs, they had been home-cooked. By my mother. I had liked them just fine.

It turned out that the ribs at this restaurant weren't anything like the ones Mom used to make, but I liked them just fine, too. So did Riel, from the way he polished them off. He pushed his plate aside, signaled for a refill on his coffee, and fished a pen and a piece of paper out of his jacket pocket.

"Tell me what she said," he said. "The exact words, if you can remember them."

I told him again, as well as I could recall.

He wrote down what I said. "That's it, just a shiny mouth?"

I nodded.

"What did she mean?"

"I don't know," I said. "She's always saying stuff like that. She said my eyes reminded her of flowers."

"Did you ask her what she meant?"

"I started to," I said. "But she said she was tired and she went inside."

He stared down at the words he had written. "Shiny mouth," he muttered. "That could be someone with braces on their teeth. A kid, maybe? Could be someone with a gold or silver cap, or several of them. Could be someone with a gold toothpick or something like that in his mouth." He sighed. "I guess it could even be a drag queen with glitter lipstick or one of those kids that hang out down on Queen, the ones with the spiky hair."

"Man, that's so old," I said. I knew there were still guys like that around. When were they going to figure out that the eighties were long gone?

He shook his head. "Did she say that she got a good look at the guy?"

I didn't know.

Riel looked at his notes again. "The man with the shiny mouth," he murmured. He peered at me again. "You sure that's what she said? *The* man with the shiny mouth, not *a* man with a shiny mouth?"

A, the? I wasn't sure.

"What difference does it make?" I asked.

"Maybe none. But think about it. She remembers a guy with a shiny mouth, she'd tell you, I saw *a* guy with a shiny mouth. But if she'd seen the guy around before somewhere and had already noticed that he had a shiny mouth, then maybe she'd think of him as *the* man with the shiny mouth. Which means maybe she knows him or could at least give a good description of him."

"Yeah," I said, and felt fluttery feathers of hope in my heart.

Riel waved for the bill.

"I'm going to take you home," he said, "then I'm going back to the hospital to check on Mrs. Jhun. Maybe she can tell us something."

"I'm coming with you."

"Mike, you've been out all day. What about your uncle?"

That was a good one. "Billy's probably not even home," I said. "So you can either take me with you, or I'll walk over on my own. Either way, I'm going back to the hospital."

He slapped some money down onto the table and didn't argue when I followed him back to the car and got in the passenger side. He'd just parked the car and we were about to get out and cross the street to the hospital when his cell phone rang. He dug into his pocket for it.

"Riel," he said. He glanced at me as he listened to whatever his caller was saying. He hit "off " and slipped the phone back into his pocket. "Sorry, Mike," was all he said.

I started to cry. I felt like a big baby sitting there, tears running down my cheeks. Riel handed me a couple of tissues.

"She was nice," I said, wiping at my tears. "She used to make me tea. I helped her paint her kitchen. I fixed her step."

Riel didn't say anything. He waited until I calmed down. Then we went into the hospital. Riel talked to one of the nurses, and then we sat in the waiting room until Dr. Thomas showed up again. Riel asked her a couple of questions.

"She never regained consciousness," he said as he was driving me home for the second time that day. "That means she wasn't in any pain, Mike."

That was good. But it also meant that she hadn't said anything to anybody about the man she had seen. That's at least one reason why Riel had wanted to talk to Dr. Thomas.

I remembered something else Mrs. Jhun had told me. "She said she wanted to be buried with Mr. Jhun," I said. "Do you think she will be?"

Riel shrugged. "I guess that depends on her family."

The house was dark when Riel pulled up in front.

"You going to be okay?" he asked me.

If he meant, was I going to be happy, no, I wasn't. I still couldn't believe she was gone. She was such a sweet old lady. But would I survive? Sure. I'd got through worse. It wasn't easy. It stung and burned and ached all at the same time. But—

"Yeah," I said. I got out of the car. Then, I couldn't help it, I ducked down to ask, "So is that the end of it? Nothing else anyone can do?"

"About Mrs. Jhun?"

"About Mom."

"I said I'd look into it, Mike."

"But you already told me your friends are too busy."

"I'm not too busy," he said. "And I've got a lot more friends. See you at school, Mike. And do your homework, okay?"

CHAPTER TEN

It was an all-round lousy weekend. I hung out near Jen's house on Sunday morning, hoping to catch her. After about an hour, I saw one of her neighbors peeking out from behind the curtains. The guy was probably a heartbeat away from calling the cops on me, so I took off. I tried phoning her from a pay phone, but her mother answered, so I hung up. I figured there was maybe half a chance that her mother would say something to Jen and Jen would know it was me who had called and she'd try to contact me, so I raced home and sat around there for a couple of hours. The phone didn't ring even once.

Billy dragged himself out of bed at around three in the afternoon. I hadn't seen him since he'd dropped me off on Saturday morning. When I told him what had happened to Mrs. Jhun, it took him a long time to even figure out who I was talking about. To top it off, neither Vin nor Sal was allowed to leave the house. Sal was still pretty much under house arrest. Vin was doubly busted because he had gone out Friday night when he was supposed to have been in his room. Billy said I was lucky. He said he'd never ground me, no matter what I did. It never accomplished anything, he said. My mom had grounded him a couple of times a week, he said, and look how much good it had done her, not to mention how much good it had done him.

I did all of my homework that night.

» » »

I stopped by Riel's desk on the way out of history class.

"Nice to see your assignment on my desk first time I asked," he said. He actually smiled at me. Then he got serious. "You holding up okay?"

I nodded. I wanted to ask him if he'd found out anything but figured it was probably too soon.

"I've got some appointments after school, Mike," he said. "Maybe I'll drop by your place later, okay?"

» » »

Big surprise. Billy was home when I got there. Dan and Lew were with him on the porch, feet up on the railing.

"Got any cupcakes, Mike?" Lew said. He loved to tease me about getting busted. "I sure love cupcakes."

"How's the girlfriend?" Dan asked. "Is it true she's rich?"

I glowered at both of them.

"Mike's best friend died," Billy said.

"Jeez," Dan said. He sounded shocked.

"She had a stroke," Billy said. "It was that old Chinese woman—"

"Korean," I corrected. Couldn't he ever get it straight?

"She was, like, seventy-five or something," Billy said.

Lew laughed. Dan didn't. He jabbed Lew with his elbow.

"Sorry to hear it, Mikey," he said. "Really."

I pushed open the rickety screen door and went inside to see if there was anything to eat.

"Hey," said Billy. He'd come in behind me.

I rummaged through the kitchen cupboards. Something definitely had to be done about the food situation around here.

"You see the paper today?" Billy said.

Was he kidding? I hardly ever read the paper. Neither did he. Billy wasn't big on reading, unless it was the big number in the corner of paper money or the label on a bottle of beer.

"There was an article about your friend," he said.

Okay, now he had my attention. I turned from the cupboard to look at him.

"I know you didn't like Mrs. Jhun," I said. "But I did, Billy. So lay off, okay?"

"Whoa," he said. He held up his hands, like he needed to protect himself from me. "I don't mean her. I'm talking about that guy Riel. It says in the paper that you and Riel found the old lady in her house."

"Yeah? So?" I abandoned the cupboard and crossed to the fridge.

"Why are you hanging around with that guy, Mike?"

I shut the fridge in disgust.

"Jeez, Billy, would it kill you to buy a few groceries every now and then? A guy could starve to death around here." I thought about the steak and salad I had seen Riel make. Mom used to make me eat salads all the time. I'd forgotten how good they tasted.

"I asked you a question, Mike."

"I'm not hanging around with him," I said. "He's my history teacher."

"Right. And you and him just happened to be at that old lady's house at the same time. It was pure coincidence, right?"

"I already told you. I've been trying to get him to look into what happened to Mom."

"You ever heard that expression, let sleeping dogs lie?" Billy said, all annoyed. "Nancy's gone. She's been gone a long time now. Besides, what can Riel do? The guy isn't even a cop anymore. Worse. He's a coward. You shouldn't hang around him."

"What do you mean, a coward?" I asked.

"He used to be a cop, now he's not a cop. What do you think I mean?" When I still didn't get it, he said, "Don't you ever wonder about stuff, Mikey? Didn't you ask yourself how come a guy who used to be a cop is teaching school now?"

I had wondered, sort of.

"It made the news a couple of years ago," Billy said. "Him and his partner, they were going into this apartment after some guy. Riel's partner was supposed to go in first. Riel was the backup guy. So his partner busts down the door and the guy inside starts shooting and, guess what? Riel just stands there. Doesn't get even one shot off. His partner goes down. Then Riel goes down. Next thing you know, Riel's not a cop anymore."

"No way," I said. No way Riel would just stand there.

"It was in the papers, Mike."

"The papers get things wrong sometimes," I said. At least, that's what people said. They must have got this wrong, too. Riel wasn't the kind of guy who would let his partner get killed and not do a thing about it.

"Come on, Mike. The guy doesn't look like more than—what—thirty-five? Guys don't retire from the cops that young. They leave because they can't cut it. Or because they get pushed out."

"Like you're an expert all of a sudden," I said.

"Ask him," Billy said. "Next time you two are rescuing old ladies, ask him."

I didn't bother pointing out that we hadn't succeeded in rescuing Mrs. Jhun.

Billy went back out on the porch. A little while later he left with Dan and Lew, which was fine by me.

I took my backpack outside and pulled out my history book. I even opened it to the right page. But I couldn't make myself focus long enough to read the pages Riel had assigned.

Around nine o'clock a car pulled up in front of the house. I recognized it right away, only now I wasn't sure I was glad to see it. Riel got out and came up the walk toward me.

"Your uncle home?" he asked.

I shook my head. A look crossed Riel's face. He seemed annoyed.

"Mind if I sit down?" he said.

There were three folding chairs all in a row where Billy and Dan and Lew had been sitting. I was in one of them now. Riel took another one and set it down so that it was opposite mine, not next to it.

"Mrs. Jhun's niece called me this evening," he said. "The funeral is on Wednesday." He fished a piece of paper out of his pocket and handed it to me. I read what was written on it, the name of a Korean church in the neighborhood. "Eleven o'clock," he said. "Get Billy to write you a note so you can get off school."

I nodded.

Riel leaned forward so his arms were resting on his knees. He looked so hard at me that I felt myself squirming and started putting my books away to cover myself.

"Problem, Mike?" he asked.

I shook my head again.

"You don't look too happy."

"It's nothing."

He studied me a moment longer.

"What do you know about the robbery at the Jhuns' restaurant?"

"Mr. Jhun got killed. Money was stolen."

"I know a guy who was working robbery when it happened," Riel said. "The place wasn't broken into. Did you know that?"

"No."

"The Jhuns lived on top of the restaurant. Mrs. Jhun told the police that the restaurant closed just after midnight. She and Mr. Jhun locked up the place and went upstairs. She says he woke up in the middle of the night—he told her he had heard something downstairs. He went downstairs, and within half a minute, two minutes at the most, Mrs. Jhun said she heard him call out. By the time she got downstairs, he was bleeding to death near the cash register. The back door was open, but it hadn't been forced."

"You mean, Mr. Jhun let the guy in?"

Riel shook his head. "I don't think so," he said. "The way the place is set up, just behind the counter near the cash register, there's a door that leads to the stairs. The stairs lead to the second-floor apartment. The cash register is about twenty-five feet from the front door, which was locked tight, from the inside, and, I don't know, maybe sixty-five feet from the back door that leads into the alley."

It was a lot of details.

"Mr. Jhun went downstairs and cried out almost at once. The theory is, he didn't have enough time to go to the back door, open it, let someone in, then struggle with that person and end up back at the cash register before Mrs. Jhun got there. She says she ran for the stairs as soon as she heard him cry out. She didn't even think about her own safety. And as soon as she saw what had happened, she called 911."

"I don't get it," I said.

"Mr. Jhun locked up the place. Front door, back door. Mrs. Jhun was there. She saw him do it. She tried the doors. She told the police she always tried the locks, ever since she found out how much money he was keeping around the place. But there was no sign of forced entry, and Mr. Jhun couldn't have let the intruder in—at least, that's what the robbery guys think. There wasn't enough time."

"What are you saying? Whoever did it had a key to the place?"

He looked deep into my eyes.

"Did you know that your mother had a key?"

"What?" What was he saying? "You're saying my mother had something to do with this?"

"I'm just asking a question, Mike."

Sure he was. He was just asking a question that was getting my mother all messed up in something I knew she couldn't have done.

"Who said she had a key?"

"*She* did. Did you know about it?"

I felt the same way I had felt when I woke up in Billy's car the other night, dizzy and sick to my stomach and afraid to open my eyes because, if I did, everything would start to spin.

"She made a statement, Mike. She signed it. I saw it."

I stood up fast, sending the stupid folding chair skittering out behind me.

The only movement Riel made was to tilt his head a little so that he could look at me.

"The Jhuns lived right above the restaurant. Mr. Jhun wanted a safe place to keep his set of spare keys, so he entrusted it to your mother. She did bookkeeping for him, right?" I nodded. "So he trusted her. At least, that's what your mother said. Mrs. Jhun told the police the same thing. She had keys to the place."

"And you think she—"

"The reason she made a statement to the police, Mike, was that Mrs. Jhun told the cops about the spare keys and they asked your mother to account for them."

"You mean, Mrs. Jhun thought Mom—"

Riel shook his head. "Not according to what she told the police. I think she trusted your mother, Mike. She was just answering questions, that's all. You know, how many keys were there to this lock? Where are they? Who had access to them?"

Who had access to them . . .

"They talked to your mom, too. They asked her whether she still had the keys the Jhuns had given her. And she said yes, and produced them. And they asked her the same questions they asked Mrs. Jhun."

He looked at me for maybe a minute. It was creepy how he could do that, be perfectly still, just look at you and make you think, man, here it comes.

"What she told them was, there's just me and my son, and he's eleven years old."

I couldn't move.

"Your mother was well-liked by just about everybody. She impressed the detectives who were investigating the case. She answered questions directly. She produced the keys. Why wouldn't anyone believe her? Did you know about it, Mike?"

I shook my head. I knew that she did work for Mr. Jhun. I knew that she kept some papers and things—she never said what things—in the box in one of her dresser drawers, under her sweaters. I knew because I had seen her put the box there. But I didn't know what was in it until after she died, when Billy went through it. I had never opened it or even touched it when Mom was alive because if I had and my mother had found out, she would have been disappointed in me. Not mad at me. But disappointed that I hadn't respected her privacy. And Mom's disappointment was a hundred times worse than her anger.

"The thing is, Mike, I've been wondering."

Here it comes.

"Do you have any idea where Billy was that night?"

I couldn't move.

"The cops never looked at him," Riel said. "Never had reason to. Your mother never mentioned him. He wasn't living in the house. He didn't hang around the restaurant, so Mrs. Jhun never mentioned him. And, far as I've been able to figure, nobody asked you about the robbery, am I right?"

I nodded.

"Because who would think an eleven-year-old would have a fix on a robbery-turned-murder." He leaned forward and straightened the chair I had knocked over. "Sit down, Mike."

I stayed where I was. Riel didn't press the point.

"I'd never have thought of it myself if you hadn't told me what your mom said to Billy," he said.

My stomach churned so hard I was sure I was going to be sick. All I had wanted to know was who had been driving the car that had killed my mom, and all Riel had done was turn Billy into a suspect in a completely different crime.

"Billy was here that night," I said.

Riel didn't look surprised. Maybe that was because he wasn't, or maybe it was because he was so good about hiding what he was thinking.

"It was a long time ago, Mike. You sure about that?"

"He slept in my room. I remember when I woke up that morning, Mom was all upset because of what had happened to Mr. Jhun." I sure remembered her being upset. "I remember Billy was there. He read me stories before bed. He always did when he stayed over."

"You're sure?"

I said I was.

"Did Billy stay over often?"

I shook my head. Around that time, he hardly ever came to the house. And whenever he did show up, he and Mom almost always got into a fight, like the time after that when Billy bought me that Xbox and Mom made him take it back. But I wasn't going to tell Riel that.

"And anyway," I said, "what does the robbery have to do with anything? My mother wasn't at the restaurant that night. She didn't know anything about that."

Riel sighed. He ran a hand through his hair.

"Maybe nothing," he said. He sighed again. "I have another piece of information."

I didn't think I wanted to hear anymore.

"I talked to another guy I know in robbery. Auto theft."

I remembered he had told me there was a good possibility that the car that killed my mother had been stolen.

"Some cars, when they get stolen, they're shipped across the country or even out of the country for sale. These days, it's amazing how far a car stolen in North America can get. The other thing that happens is they get chopped—you know, taken apart—and the parts are sold instead of the whole vehicle. It can be pretty lucrative. So this guy I know in robbery, he tells me that maybe that's why we weren't able to recover the Impala that was involved in the accident. He says it's possible it could have been chopped and sold for parts, maybe as soon as the day after the accident."

"So that's the end of that?" I said.

He shrugged, and left me wondering why he had even bothered to tell me.

"I could ask my friend in robbery to look around some more. See if he knows anybody who knows anything—you know, anything they have on chop shops that might have been operating in the area at the time, anyone with any record relating to disposing of stolen cars. There's still lots of ways to go at it. There just isn't any more I can tell you right now."

Yeah, there was.

"Why'd you quit the cops?"

Finally, the impossible-to-read expression slipped from his face.

"That's a long story," he said quietly.

"Billy says it's because you're a coward." It was mean, and I only said it because I was mad at him. Because he had asked all those questions that made it seem like somehow my mom had something to do with what had happened to Mr. Jhun. And because now he was telling me that the main evidence in the case was never going to be found. The car that had killed my mother had either been sold half a world away or chopped into parts. Either way, it was gone, gone, gone.

Maybe I was mad, but Riel wasn't. I guess I expected him to yell at me—how dare I say such a thing? For sure I had expected him to deny it. He didn't.

"I guess that's an opinion," he said. "I was supposed to be backing up my partner. Something went wrong. I didn't want that to happen again." He stood up slowly. "I really am sorry I couldn't bring you any good news, Mike."

I watched him go down the walk and climb into his car. I felt bad about what I had said, but once you've said something, you can't take it back. It lies out there like a big, ripe old piece of garbage, stinking up the neighborhood.

CHAPTER ELEVEN

I was sprawled on the couch watching Conan O'Brien when Billy came in. He smelled like cigarettes, which meant he had probably been at his favorite sports bar. He stood in the entrance to the living room. I knew he was watching me, not expecting me to say hello. I ignored him.

"Hey, kid," he said, "don't you have school tomorrow?"

"Since when do you care?"

"Whoa!" Billy grinned. He was standing in the doorway between the living room and the front hall. "What flew up your nose and bit you?"

"Riel was here," I said.

"I warned you about that guy." He shook his finger at me, like a not-very-serious kindergarten teacher scolding a mischievous little kid, except there was an edge to his voice and his beery eyes got a little sharper.

"He said stuff about Mom. And he was asking about you, Billy."

"Yeah?" He came into the living room and gave my legs a kick so I'd make room for him on the couch. "What was he asking about?"

"He wanted to know where you were the night Mr. Jhun was killed."

"Why'd he want to know that?" he said. Man, did he look mad. "And, anyway, I was here."

"I know. I told him that."

"Good boy, Mikey." He peered at me. "Is there something else?"

I hesitated. "The way he was talking, I think he thinks Mom had something to do with what happened at the restaurant. Or that you did. She had keys to the place. Did you know that?"

"Keys to what place?"

"To the Jhuns' place. Did you know about that, Billy?"

He shook his head.

"Riel says she had keys. He said it like he was blaming her for what happened." But maybe that wasn't fair. He'd also said that she had answered all the questions. He'd said she was well-liked. He had made it seem like the police had believed her. But then he had said, "Why shouldn't they?" What did that mean?

"Don't be an idiot, Mike," Billy said. "Nancy was always a good girl. She would never do anything wrong. You should go to bed."

I didn't move. The whole time I'd been sitting here, I'd been wondering about what Riel had said: *I could ask my friend to look into it more.* Did that mean he was going to do it, or did I have to ask him to? Did he care all on his own, or would he only agree to care, well, sort of, if I kept pushing it?

"There's something else, Billy."

I had to talk this one out with someone. I had to get a read on it.

Billy waited.

"Mom's case isn't closed. He said, if they're not solved, they're not closed. He thinks maybe there's a way to find out who killed Mom. To find out what happened to the car, anyway. He says maybe that could get them somewhere."

"Jeez, Mike!" Billy shook his head. "It's been four years. We've been through this already."

"But he's pretty sure that the car that hit her was stolen. He says either it was shipped out of town or it was cut up for parts, probably the very next day. He said one minute you have a brand-new Impala, the next minute all you have is a bunch of parts that get sold and a car that never gets found because even though the cops put out a description of it, the car thieves aren't going to come forward. But he knows guys, you know, from the auto squad."

"Go to bed, Mike," Billy said. He said it nicely. Later, when I was lying in bed, I thought I heard the front door open and then close again and a lock turn in the key. It was two in the morning. Where was Billy going?

» » »

I was glad I didn't have history the next day, because I don't think I could have faced Riel. Not after what he had said. Not after what I had said. I kept my head down and tried to at least look like I was doing my work. On my way home, when I got close to Mr. Scorza's store, I crossed the street so that he wouldn't see me and I wouldn't see him. I felt like I was hiding from everyone, like I had turned into the world's biggest coward.

When I got home, Billy was standing at the kitchen sink. For a guy who had told me to get some sleep, he didn't look like he'd even come close to taking his own advice.

"Hey, Billy," I said. I prayed there was some peanut butter left and maybe a couple of slices of bread. I didn't even care how old they were. I was starving.

"I gotta talk to you, Mikey."

"You gotta shave, Billy. Have you seen yourself lately?"

"I want you to talk to this guy Riel," Billy said. "I want you to get him to back off, stop him asking any more questions. Tell him you decided you don't want to know. Tell him it's bringing up too many bad memories."

What? Was he crazy?

"No way. Besides, I don't even want to talk to him right now." I didn't want him to back off, either.

"Guys like him, Mikey, when they start asking questions, especially if they're asking cops, they can stir up a lot of trouble."

"Trouble for whoever killed Mom," I said.

“Maybe trouble for other people, too,” Billy said. His whole body was tense. One hand was clenched around the neck of a beer bottle. The other was picking at the label.

“What’s the matter with you, Billy?”

“Jeez, Mike, why do you have to be so stubborn? You’re just like Nancy. You get an idea in your head and you don’t let it rest. Now look what you’ve gone and done.”

What? What had I gone and done?

“Don’t you care what happened?” I asked. But the truth mostly was, no, he didn’t. All Billy ever cared about was Billy. “She was my mother, and if I want to know what happened, I have a right.”

“What’d you have to go poking a stick into that cage for?” he said.

“You’re drunk, Billy.” I decided right then to ignore him. Let him ramble on. Let him say whatever he wanted, I wasn’t going to listen. All I wanted was to get past him, make a sandwich and get out of the kitchen.

Billy grabbed me. “I mean it. You got to make him stop.”

His hand bit into my forearm. Big mistake. I wasn’t in the mood for this. And just because Billy was older, that didn’t mean he was bigger or tougher. In fact, my dad must have been way taller than his because, minus the heels on his boots, the top of Billy’s head only came to the top of my nose. Plus he had been drinking. Plus he sat around too much with his loser friends, so he wasn't in great shape. I grabbed the thumb that was digging into my forearm and wrenched it back until Billy howled.

"You don't care what really happened to Mom, that's fine with me," I said. It wasn't fine, though. It made me want to keep wrenching Billy's thumb until it snapped right off. "But *I* care. I care so much you'd practically have to kill me to make me stop. So butt out, Billy, okay?"

Billy's knees must have all of a sudden given way, because one minute he was standing and the next he plunked down into one of the kitchen chairs. I let go of him.

"Just stay out of my way," I said.

"You don't know where this is going, Mikey."

"Yeah? And you do?"

He looked down at the floor, or maybe at the toes of his boots.

"I saw the car," he said.

I heard him say the words. I saw his mouth move, so I knew for a fact that they came out of his mouth. But I still didn't believe he had said it.

"I didn't know it was the one, though," he said. He finally raised his head. He didn't look good. His face was kind of crumpled, like it was caving in on itself. His eyes were red—probably from the beer, I told myself, but maybe not. He looked a few centuries older than he really was.

"What do you mean, you saw it?" Was that really my voice? So quiet, so calm, like, hey, I had everything under control, no problem. It didn't seem possible because inside I felt a white heat. It burned in my stomach, in my head, in my heart.

"I swear I didn't know it was the same car," he said. "It wasn't the color they said, not that it would have made any difference. They didn't say anything about the color or the make until it was too late."

He knew something. My Uncle Billy knew something about the car that had killed his sister—my mother.

"That guy pokes around anymore or gets guys from the auto squad to poke around anymore in that direction, he's gonna find out stuff that's going to put me in a spot, Mikey."

The words formed in my brain. I could see them. Taste them. But it took forever before I could bring myself to spit them out.

"You were involved?"

Say no. Come on, Billy. Convince me. Say you had nothing to do with it.

Billy's head sagged. He stared at the crumb-speckled tabletop. Slowly he shook his head.

"Billy?"

His head came up. His eyes were watery. Tears?

"Did I have anything to do with what happened to Nancy? No," he said. But I knew, I could feel it, there was something he wasn't saying. Something big.

"But?" I said it softly, like I cared that this was hard for him, when really I wanted to beat him over the head with the word.

His shoulders sagged. He was smaller and older than I had ever seen him.

"It's not cheap living in this city," he said. "Some people got more money than they know what to do with, and some are just scraping by."

I waited. The kitchen had grown very cold, the way the whole house had after Mom died.

"It was no big deal," he said. "It wasn't like I was some kind of criminal mastermind or anything."

I started to get a bad feeling in my stomach. A sick feeling, like at Vin's cousin's party.

"I just put in a few hours of overtime, that's all. A few lousy hours. A little muscle, that's all."

"What do you mean, overtime?"

No answer.

"Jeez, Billy!"

"Sometimes, at night, someone would bring in a car and I'd work on it. You know."

I shook my head.

"Strip it down," he said. "You know, for parts."

"You mean, like a chop shop?"

"Jeez, no, nothing like that. Sometimes, *occasionally*, if I was working late, I'd find a car out back, and if I put the time in and busted it down, I could make some good money. Strictly cash."

"You took apart stolen cars, is that what you're telling me, Billy?"

"Nobody ever said they were stolen," he said. He was like a kid: I didn't know they were your Lego blocks when I took them, I thought someone just left them lying there. "Mostly they were guys who just wanted a new car. They'd report their car stolen, then they'd arrange to deliver it to the garage and we'd take it apart for them. Help them make sure it would never be recovered. We'd split with them what we got for the parts. They'd collect from the insurance company and get a new car. Everyone was happy. No one got hurt."

"We?"

"The guy I used to work for. He's gone now. Out of the country."

I looked at my uncle and thought I had never seen a more pathetic human being in my life. I always knew Billy was no genius. If you'd pushed me, I would have said that he was flat-out lazy. Always looking for the easy way. Never putting himself out if there was someone else around to do the work. But this?

"Billy, are you telling me that you took apart the car that—" My throat was so dry it choked me. I couldn't make myself finish the sentence.

"When the cops came out with the information, they said green," Billy said. "They said the car that killed Nancy was a dark green Impala. And they never said anything about stolen—" He stopped and looked at me. I think he realized he'd said the wrong word. He'd just admitted that he knew that at least some of the cars he was *taking apart*, as he put it, were stolen. "All I know is, this car was waiting out back, it was black, not green, and I took it apart." He kept his eyes on the floor. "The paint job was new. But I swear I didn't even think until later . . ." His voice trailed off.

"You know who probably left it there, don't you?" I said. What I was thinking was, *the guy who ran down my mother.*

"I didn't see anyone," Billy said. "I never saw anyone. I just did a job, that's all."

"What about the robbery? Did you have anything to do with the robbery at Mr. Jhun's restaurant?" Even if he said no, I wasn't sure I was going to believe him. Mom had the second key. The place hadn't been forcibly broken into. Whoever had killed Mr. Jhun had probably let himself in with a key. That's what the police had said.

Billy looked me square in the face. "No," he said. "I don't know anything about that. And I didn't have anything to do with Nancy getting killed, I swear it to you, Mikey. But here's the thing. If the cops start digging around or if you breathe a word of this to Riel, it's all gonna fall on me. It's not going to help them find out who killed Nancy. But it's gonna mean serious time for me, Mikey. They'll put me away for sure. And I didn't do anything."

"Except destroy the evidence," I said. "And make it impossible for them to find Mom's killer."

"I swear I didn't know," he said. "Jeez, Mike, you think I'd do anything to help my sister's killer get away with it?"

Did he ever listen to himself? I wondered.

"Isn't that what you're doing now?" I said.

"I'm the same as you, Mike. I want whoever killed Nancy to pay. But I don't know who did it. I don't know anything. All I know is that if they link me to that car, and if they look into what I was doing a couple of years ago, I'm in the biggest trouble of my life. I'll go to jail," he said. More like he whined it. "Is that what you want?"

I stared at my uncle, the man I had been living with, who had supposedly been looking after me for the past four years. Stared at him and, for the first time, saw a big cowardly kid.

"How's it gonna help?" Billy said. "It's not going to change what happened to Nancy. You don't want me to go to prison, do you, Mikey? If I do, what'll happen to you? You want to be in foster care? Is that what you want?"

I stared at him a moment longer, then I went upstairs to my room, closed the door, and sat on my bed. I stayed there, not moving, while my room—and my world—faded from light to gray to black.

CHAPTER TWELVE

Billy wasn't home when I got up in the morning. I told myself I didn't care. I didn't want to talk to him. I didn't want to see him ever again.

I got dressed, went downstairs, and stared into the empty fridge for a few minutes. For once, though, I wasn't hungry. I wasn't anything, really. I don't think I slept. I kept thinking: all this time, Billy knew something. Billy had done something, and he had kept his mouth shut about it. Suddenly I couldn't stand to be in the house anymore. I couldn't stand the idea that I'd be standing there and Billy would walk in and I'd have to look at him.

I grabbed my backpack and headed for the door. My backpack. I looked at it. A sack of books and notes and school stuff that didn't mean anything. I threw it down and left the house.

I headed over to Jen's house and hung around out of

sight for a while, but I didn't see her. After that I walked up to Cosburn and across until I passed Woodbine. You could get into the park system there, and then you could walk and walk, all the way up to Sunnybrook Hospital if you wanted to. That's what I did. I walked and I thought.

Around ten or so, I remembered about Mrs. Jhun's funeral. I should have gone. She'd been a good friend of Mom's. She'd been a friend of mine, too. But it was too late. I was too far from my neighborhood. By the time I got there, the whole thing would be over.

I kept going. I walked so far north that I ran out of park, and still I kept walking.

I thought about going to the cops and telling them what Billy had told me. But then what? Billy was probably right. If Billy told them what he had told me—a big IF—they'd arrest him. If I told them, Billy would probably chicken out and deny it. What would happen then? The cops wouldn't just believe me, would they? They'd have to investigate. What could they possibly find out all these years later?

There had to be something. That's the thing that rooted itself in my mind. There had to be something because, otherwise, why would Billy be so worried? If there was no way the cops could find anything, why would Billy want me to get Riel to back off? Why would he even admit to me what he had done?

My brain just about exploded.

Billy was worried. He was worried because he thought the cops would uncover something if they dug deep enough. That's why he wanted me to stop Riel. And if I didn't stop Riel . . .

I stood in the middle of nowhere, shaking when I thought about it.

If Billy wanted me to stop Riel, then it could mean only one thing. Whatever Billy had done—or not done—he knew more than he had told me. He was hiding something. But what? Had he lied when he said he didn't see who had dropped off the car at the garage? Was he afraid to tell because he was afraid of what that person might do to him—more afraid than of what the police might do? Maybe it was something different from what Billy had said. Maybe he'd got mixed up in a car-theft ring. Whatever it was, I was going to get it out of him. I turned around and started walking back.

It was nearly suppertime by the time I got out of the park, and my appetite had returned. I dug in my pockets. At the first corner store I passed, I bought a meat patty and ate it in about two bites. I was hiking along Cosburn, heading home, wondering what was in the fridge, when a police cruiser slid by, going in the opposite direction. It passed me, then did a U-turn and pulled up beside me. One of the cops got out.

"What's your name, son?" he asked.

"Why?" I hadn't done anything wrong.

He didn't get mad, and there was something funny about the way he was looking at me.

"What's your name?" he said again.

I told him.

"You need to come with us, Mike," he said. "You're wanted at home."

What? Billy had called the cops on me?

"What for?" I asked.

"They'll explain it to you there," the cop said. He opened the back car door for me. "Come on, Mike."

I got in. The other cop, the one who wasn't driving, radioed that they had me. Then nobody said anything. We just rolled along Cosburn, down to Danforth and then down my street.

There was another police car outside my house, and a police truck. On the side it said Forensic Identification. I saw Riel standing on the street, talking to one of the uniformed officers. He turned when he saw the squad car and came over and opened the door for me. I forgot about being mad at him. Mostly I was glad to see him. "What are you doing here?" I said.

"I went to the funeral this morning. You didn't show up, so I came by to see if everything was okay. When I got here, they were here." He nodded at the cops.

"What's the matter?" I asked. "What's going on?"

"It's your uncle," he said.

"What about Billy?" I asked. Then, because I couldn't think of anything else that made sense, I said, "Did they arrest him?"

Riel shook his head. He led me over to his car and opened the passenger side door.

"Sit down, Mike," he said.

I sat, my legs sticking out the open door.

Riel glanced back at the house. Then he said, "Billy's dead."

I laughed. It was automatic, because the first thing that popped into my head was: this is a joke. Except that Riel didn't even crack a smile.

"I'm sorry, Mike," he said.

That's when I knew he wasn't kidding.

"But . . . what happened?" I asked.

Riel shook his head. "I don't know yet. The Ident guys are inside. And there's a couple of homicide detectives who are going to want to talk to you."

Homicide? "Someone *killed* Billy?"

"Homicide gets called whenever there's a suspicious death," Riel said. "Sometimes it turns out it was an accident or the person died of natural causes. But they have to check it out." He glanced over his shoulder. Two men in business suits were coming down the walk toward us. "They're going to want to ask you some questions, Mike. Okay?"

The two detectives introduced themselves. Detective Jones and Detective London.

"What happened to Billy?" I asked them.

"That's what we're looking into, Mike," Detective Jones said. "We're going to have to ask you a few questions, okay? You can have someone with you when we talk to you if you want. You want us to call someone?" It was only later that I realized that Detective Jones talked a lot like Riel—slowly, calmly, patiently.

There was no one I could call. I turned to Riel.

"You want me to stay, Mike?" he asked.

Neither of the detectives looked too happy about that. But Detective Jones said, "Do you want John to stay with you, Mike?"

I nodded. Then the questions started, a whole torrent of them, coming at me one right after the other. They kept asking and asking, and all I could think was, *Billy is dead. Billy. Dead.*

"When was the last time you saw your uncle?"

The last time? "Yesterday. After school." *When I was mad at him. When I thought I never wanted to speak to him again.*

"You didn't see him this morning?"

I wished I had. I thought of all the things I could have said. "He was gone when I got up."

"Was that unusual?"

I nodded my head yes. Billy was usually sprawled in his bed when I got up in the morning. Usually I had to wake him up so that he got to work on time.

"What about you, Mike? When did you leave the house today?"

"About eight, I guess."

"Where did you go?"

I told him everything I had done today. I didn't tell him I had spent the whole day thinking about Billy.

"You didn't come back here at all?" Detective Jones said.

I wished I had. I wished I had never left the house. Maybe if I had stayed home, maybe if I had talked to Billy, things would be different now.

"What can you tell us about your uncle, Mike?" he asked.

Right now, I could have told them a thousand things. Little things. Like how Billy thought hot dogs with ketchup and relish was a balanced meal—ketchup is made from tomatoes, relish from pickles, so there's your vegetables right there. Or how Billy had no clue how to do laundry—all of his white socks had turned gray because he washed them with his jeans and T-shirts. Or how Billy charmed girls by singing them the one song he had written—he just put in a different girl's name each time.

"What do you mean?" I asked.

"Was anything bothering him? Did he seem preoccupied?"

I glanced at Riel.

"Mike?" Detective Jones said. "Was something bothering your uncle?"

I shook my head. Is it a lie if you don't come right out and say the words?

"When you saw your uncle last night, how did he seem?"

"He'd been drinking," I said. An honest answer.

"Did you talk to him?"

"Yeah. A little."

"Did you notice anything out of the ordinary about him?"

Why was he asking that? Did the cops know something? Did they suspect something?

"What do you mean?" I said again.

"Maybe he was upset about something. Depressed. Anything like that?"

I glanced at Riel again. This time the two detectives exchanged glances.

"Look, Mike," Detective Jones said, "we're just trying to find out what happened to your uncle."

What had happened to him? I realized then that they hadn't actually told me. I wasn't sure that I wanted to know, but I figured I owed it to Billy to ask.

"How did he die?"

Detective Jones glanced at Riel. So did I. Riel sighed. Then he shrugged, like he knew something bad was going to happen and there was nothing he could do to stop it.

"Looks like asphyxiation," Detective Jones said.

"You mean, like he was smothered?"

There was a heartbeat of a moment before he answered.

"He was hanged, Mike."

I think my brain stopped working right then. I couldn't wrap my mind around what he had just told me. Hanged? Billy?

"You mean, he killed himself?"

"We're looking into it, Mike," Detective Jones said. "That's why we really need you to answer our questions."

"Anything you can tell the detectives about Billy might help them figure out exactly what happened," Riel said.

Billy. Hanged. That decided it.

"I saw him yesterday after school," I said. "He was in the kitchen when I got home, and he had been drinking. We talked about my mother, about how she died." This didn't seem to surprise the two detectives. Riel must have filled them in on my family background. "Billy was upset because I had been talking about it to Mr. Riel. He wanted me to just shut up about it, and I told him I wouldn't."

"Was there something in particular he didn't want you to say, Mike?"

I told them everything. There was no reason not to. Nothing worse could happen to Billy now. Nothing worse could happen to me, either.

The detectives took notes while I talked. When I had finished, they asked me a few questions. Then they asked me to go to the police station to make a statement.

"Can it wait until tomorrow?" Riel said.

They said it could. Just as they were finishing, a woman showed up. She said she was from Children's Aid.

I remembered what Billy had said to me. You want to end up in foster care, Mikey? Is that what you want? Like I was the one who was going to put me there if I didn't keep my mouth shut. Only it wasn't me who had done it. It was Billy. Billy, who was hanged.

"I'm not going with her," I told Riel.

"You have any other relatives in the city?"

I shook my head. I didn't have any other relatives, period. Riel stood there for a few moments, his hands in his pockets. Finally he said, "You want to stay at my place tonight, Mike? We can make other plans tomorrow."

I looked at the woman from Children's Aid. She was older than my mom had been, and she looked like she was going to collapse under the weight of the huge purse that hung off her shoulder. She frowned when Riel made his suggestion, but she didn't say no. Instead, she took Riel aside and talked to him. They talked for a long time. The whole time, the woman was scribbling in a folder. When she finished talking to Riel, she called one of the detectives over and talked to him and made more notes. Then she pulled out a cell phone and made a call. Finally she gave Riel her card. Then she walked back up the street to her car.

"You can't go in the house yet," Riel said to me. "If there's anything you need for tonight, you can tell Detective Jones and someone will get it for you when they can. Okay?"

I told the detective, as well as I could remember, where to find my toothbrush and my backpack and some clean clothes. Then I got into Riel's car and we drove to his house.

"You hungry, Mike?" he asked as he unlocked the front door.

I started to say that I wasn't, but by now it was way past suppertime and, except for that one patty, I hadn't eaten all day.

Riel showed me upstairs to a spare room that had a couch, a small TV, and what looked like a million books in it.

"This folds out into a bed," he said. "You'll find sheets and blankets and a pillow in the hall closet. Bathroom's second on the left. You can chill out with some TV if you want while I get dinner ready. If you want to talk—about anything at all—I'm in the kitchen, okay?"

He left the room so quietly that it took me a moment to realize that I was alone. I sank down onto the couch, reached automatically for the remote, and clicked the TV on. Right away I clicked it off again. Billy was dead. Billy, who never listened when you told him to do something, who always had a thousand excuses why he couldn't fix the screen door or hang his jacket up or spend more money on groceries than on beer. Billy, who used to take me down to the park with him when he was thirteen or fourteen and I was three or four. Who'd push me so high on the swing that I thought I was flying. Who took me into the pool with him down at Monarch Park. Who used to take me to swimming lessons when Mom was busy. He even used to read to me, although I don't remember seeing him with a book in his hands again after he was out of school. Billy, who stood right beside me at Mom's funeral, his hand on my shoulder, squeezing it, letting me know that I had to be strong, that I could get through it. He was twenty-one when Mom died. His main interests were girls, drinking, having fun, and working just hard enough to pay for all three, and there he was all of a sudden with an eleven-year-old nephew to look after and, okay, so he never actually turned into a parent, but he didn't complain, either. He never tried to pawn me off on someone else. When I played in a soccer league, when I still cared about that stuff, he was there, cheering on the sidelines. Billy. My uncle, who was more like a big brother. Billy was dead.

I looked around the room. It was like the rest of the house, clean and bare, like no one lived here, not really. I went downstairs and found Riel in the kitchen, cutting chicken into little pieces.

"You like stir-fry, Mike?"

I told him I'd never tried it. He tossed me a red pepper and a green pepper and asked me to wash them and cut them into small chunks. I was glad to have something to do. The radio was on, tuned to one of those golden oldies stations. I chopped, he cooked, and before I knew it, we were sitting at the kitchen table, eating. I surprised myself by having three helpings.

"You holding up okay?" Riel asked when the last of the stir-fry was gone.

I said I was, but it was a lie. Sure, I had wolfed down supper like there was a famine coming and everyone knew it, but I couldn't control my stomach anymore than I could control my mind. And my mind was spinning out of control. Suddenly it felt like everything I had just shoveled into my stomach was going to come spewing out again.

"It's my fault," I said. There, the thing—one of the things—that had been gnawing at me was out in the open. "If I hadn't started bugging you about what happened to Mom, Billy wouldn't have got all nervous. He wouldn't have told me what he did. You should have seen him, Mr. Riel."

"John," Riel said. "My name is John."

"I don't know whether he was ashamed or afraid or

both, but he was feeling bad, that was for sure."

Riel got up and started to clear the table. I couldn't tell whether he was listening to me or not. He messed around at the sink for a while, then he said, "You're going to have to think about what happens next."

"What do you mean?"

"There must be someone, Mike. A grandmother, a second cousin, someone who's family."

I shook my head. "Mom and Billy, they were it. My dad died a few years back, and besides, I never knew him. If he had any family, I don't know about it. Anyway, they'd be complete strangers to me."

Riel cleaned out the sink, then washed his hands and dried them on a towel that was hanging inside one of the cupboard doors.

"I have some papers to mark, Mike," he said. "But they can wait if you want to talk."

But I didn't. Not then, anyway. I told him I was tired, which was true. I had spent the whole day walking. I went upstairs, made up the bed, and turned on the TV. It was maybe ten o'clock when I heard the doorbell. I clicked down the volume on the TV, crept to the door of the spare room, and opened it.

"Jonesy," Riel was saying.

"Brought the kid's stuff by," a voice said. I recognized it. It was Detective Jones. "How's he doing?"

"Okay," Riel said. Then, "He's a good kid."

Boy, if I had a nickel for every time someone had said that about me lately, I'd have, well, a nickel.

"How about you, Johnny? How are you doing?"

"You think homicide is a hard gig? You should try teaching high school," Riel said. "You got anything yet?"

"You know I can't say."

"Used to be you'd tell me everything," Riel said. It was so quiet for the next few seconds that I thought maybe Detective Jones had left. Then he spoke. "From what the kid said, it sounds like maybe his uncle had reason enough—guilt, remorse, shame, fear of discovery, you name it."

"What about the note?"

"It was brief, that's for sure. Three words—*Sorry for everything.* The handwriting guys are taking a look at it. Then there's the front door, him leaving it open like that. When a guy kills himself, he usually has a pretty good idea who's going to find him. You know how they plan these things, John. He would have figured the kid would come home after school and find him, right? But he doesn't want that. He doesn't want it to be the kid, so instead he leaves the front door wide open and a neighbor's dog runs in, and then the neighbor comes in. Spares the kid the scene. Anyway, the postmortem's scheduled for tomorrow morning. Guess we'll know for sure then."

They talked for another minute, lame stuff, nothing important. I waited until the door closed, then I went downstairs.

If Riel was surprised to see me, he sure hid it well. He handed me my backpack and a bag of stuff—my toothbrush, some clothes, a picture in a frame. I pulled it out and looked at it. It was the picture that usually sat on my dresser—my mom, me when I was three or four, and Billy at thirteen or fourteen. I looked at it and my eyes got all watery.

Maybe I heard the doorbell again later that night and maybe I just dreamed I did. Maybe I heard a woman's voice downstairs and maybe I didn't.

CHAPTER THIRTEEN

I guess I must have got some sleep, because I don't remember every single minute of that night I spent in Riel's spare room. But I know I was awake by about five in the morning, and at six, when I heard noises in the kitchen and smelled coffee, I dressed and headed downstairs.

Riel was sitting at the kitchen table, drinking coffee. It was still dark out. This time of year, the sun didn't really get going until almost seven. But Riel hadn't bothered to turn on a light. He was sitting in the dark.

"You're up early," he said.

"Couldn't sleep."

"There's juice in the fridge. Or milk." He peered through the gloom at me. "Unless you drink coffee."

"Juice is fine," I said. Then, when he started to get up, "I'll get it."

I poured myself a glass and came back to the table. We sat in silence for a few moments. Then Riel said,

"It's not your fault, Mike."

"Yeah, but if I hadn't—"

"I knew you'd tell Billy," he said. His hands were wrapped tightly around his mug of coffee, like the temperature had dropped to forty below and that mug was his only source of heat. "That's why I told you, Mike." He spoke slowly, quietly. "After what you told me, I couldn't shake the feeling that there was some link between Billy and what happened to your mother, only I didn't know what it was. I figured if I tipped my hand, you'd tell Billy. Then one of two things would happen."

I felt something big and ugly come alive in my gut.

"Was Billy killing himself one of those things?"

Riel shook his head. "Believe me, Mike, if I'd had any idea—" His knuckles were white against the deep blue of the mug. "I figured that if he thought we were taking another look"—*we* again, like he'd forgotten he wasn't a cop anymore—"I figured he'd either run to whoever he was working with, or he'd do nothing because there was nothing to do, because he wasn't involved."

I stared at him a moment. This was a person I had trusted—well, sort of. I'd told him what I knew. I'd been straight with him.

"So," I said, trying to digest the words before spitting them back out at him, "basically, you used me."

"If I'd had any idea—"

I stood up. I wanted to go home. Now. But what was home anymore except a rickety, empty old house? There wasn't anyone there anymore. I felt like throwing something, maybe the toaster oven that sat on the counter, throwing it right through the kitchen window, listening to the shatter of glass, listening to the *clink-clink* as it hit the ground outside. I felt like kicking something, breaking something, shoving my fist through the wall, flying across the table at Riel, punching him, hurting him.

Riel stood up, too, but slowly, looking at me the whole time.

"We have to go downtown later," he said. "You have to make a statement. You want me to come with you, or you want me to arrange for someone else?"

Someone else? Like my life was full of someone elses.

"That lady from Children's Aid," I said to him. "You think she'd do it?"

I was glad for the pinch of surprise on his face: I don't want you, I want someone else, anyone else, a complete stranger would be a big improvement.

He checked the clock on the wall. "It's too early now, but I'll call her as soon as I can. You want something to eat?"

I shook my head. I didn't want anything from him. I went back upstairs, closed the door, and flipped through TV channels until Riel came upstairs and I heard the shower run. While he was in the bathroom I went back downstairs and made myself a peanut butter sandwich. The newspaper was lying open on the kitchen counter. I scanned the page. *Man, 25, found dead in home.* The article gave Billy's name, William James Wyatt. It said that he had been found dead, that the police were still investigating and that they weren't making any statements at this time. It said Billy worked as a garage mechanic. That's all it said.

Riel called the woman from Children's Aid and arranged to have her meet me at police headquarters. Then he called the school and said that I wouldn't be in today and that he would be late. He drove me downtown. The Children's Aid woman—she introduced herself as Margaret Phillips—was standing on the sidewalk outside. She smiled at me and asked me to wait a minute while she spoke to Riel. I don't know what they talked about, and I didn't care. Riel drove away and Margaret Phillips and I went up the steps and through the doors to the front desk. We were taken upstairs, and I sat down with her and with Detective Jones and I told them the whole story again—when I had last seen Billy, what he had been like then, what we had talked about, what he had told me, where he had gone after that and where I had gone. They let me tell the whole thing in my own words. After that, Detective Jones asked me some questions. And that was that.

"I want to go to school," I told Ms. Phillips when we left police headquarters.

"But, Mike, don't you think—"

We discussed it, and finally she said I could go. On the way there, she told me that she was going to find foster parents for me. She said she'd pick me up after school and help me get settled.

Get settled.

Like I could ever feel settled again. And settled where, exactly? I didn't have any relatives. There had been nobody except Billy. So now what was going to happen? Was I supposed to settle with people I didn't even know, people who were going to get paid to look after me, foster parents who would just be counting the days until I turned eighteen?

Settled. Right.

It was lunchtime by the time she dropped me off. She told me where she'd be waiting for me after school and gave me four quarters and a card with her phone number on it.

"If it gets to be too much, call me," she said. "Anytime, Mike. Even if it's five minutes from now. I'll come and get you. Okay?"

I told her okay. Then I headed around to the back of the school to look for Vin and Sal. Sure enough, I spotted Vin at the far end of the football field. He was turned half away from me, so he didn't see me. I had just started across the field when someone called my name. Jen. I turned. She waited for my eyes to meet hers, then she walked toward me until I could count the freckles on her nose and smell that perfume she always wore. I closed my eyes for a moment, waiting to see if she'd slip her arms around me and hug me close, like she used to.

She didn't. She stopped a couple of feet away from me and stood her ground. Her green eyes glistened with tears.

"I heard about your uncle," she said. Her voice quivered, and I thought maybe that was a good sign. If she cared about what had happened to Billy, maybe she cared about what was going to happen to me, too. "Oh, Mike, I'm so sorry. How did he . . . ?" She stopped. She couldn't bring herself to say the word.

"They're not sure yet," I said. I wanted to catch her in my arms, pull her close, and feel the warmth of her skin and the tickle of her breath on my face. But she hung back, just out of reach, and I remembered what a jerk I had been the last time I'd seen her.

"How are you doing?" she said. Her coppery eyebrows were pulled tight over her eyes, accenting her concern. "Where are you staying?"

I shrugged. An as-yet-unresolved question.

"You want to do something later, Jen?" I said. "I could use some company."

She looked away for a moment. A couple of faint lines creased her smooth forehead.

"Mike, I'd really like to. I can't even imagine how bad you must feel."

But. There was a but coming. I could see it and feel it and taste it. She was trying to be nice, though, so she didn't say it.

"Busy, huh?" I said at last.

She seemed to shrink as she shrugged her narrow shoulders.

"Patrick, huh?"

Her eyes slipped away from mine and stayed fixed on the ground for so long I thought she was never going to look at me again.

"It's not what you think, Mike," she said. "It's—" She broke off. Her eyes met mine. "If you want me to, I'll spend as much time with you as you want."

A minute ago, I would have been in heaven to hear her say that. I watched her wipe away a tear. Right then I think she would have done anything for me. She would have done it because it was what I wanted. Me. Not her. She would have done it out of pity. Poor Mike.

"I'm so sorry about Billy," she said.

"Thanks." I could have held out my arms. If I had wanted her to, she would have hugged me. "Thanks, Jen," I said. I glanced over my shoulder and saw Vin watching me. My best friend Vin. "Look," I said, "I gotta go." I turned right away, so I wouldn't catch the expression on her face, wouldn't have to see if she looked relieved. I walked across the field to Vin, who slapped me on the back and said, "Mom says you can stay with us for a while."

I felt like kissing him. His mom, too.

"You want to ditch the afternoon?" he asked. "We can go downtown, catch a movie. I know this guy who's a ticket taker at—"

I shook my head.

"I'm going to take a walk, Vin," I said. I had come to school thinking that if I could just be with people, the ache might fade a little. But Jen didn't want me and Vin—well, Vin was my best friend and a great guy, but he wasn't what I needed. "Catch up with you later, okay?"

He didn't argue with me. He never did.

» » »

Going to school had been a dumb idea. I couldn't concentrate. To be honest, if I had been quizzed on exactly which classes I went to that afternoon—never mind what the teachers had talked about—even if my life had depended on it, I couldn't have answered. Every time the bell rang, I moved from where I had been to somewhere else. I took a seat. I opened a notebook. I heard voices. But I didn't listen. I didn't write. I didn't understand. I didn't care.

Mom was gone. Billy was gone. There was only me. It was a weird feeling. Scary. One minute you have a family, the next minute you're all alone in the world. Who was I going to have Christmas dinner with? Who on the planet could say, Man, I've known you since the day you were born? Billy used to say it all the time. *Mikey, you can't snow me, I've known you since the day you were born.* Who could tell me about the day I had taken my first step or lost my first tooth? Mom probably cared more about those things than Billy ever did, but Billy had known about them, too. He liked to tease Mom that I had walked to him before I had walked to her. Who could tell me, When you do that, you remind me of your father or mother or uncle? Who was going to put up with me when I was in a bad mood? Okay, so maybe Billy used to lose his cool sometimes when I was being a jerk. But he didn't say, That's it, I'm outta here, we're through. He was always there. Because he had to be there. Because he was family. He was all the family I had.

Instead of sticking around after school to meet Ms. Phillips like I had promised, I slipped out a side exit and headed home.

I knew I probably wasn't going to be able to go inside. Sure enough, yellow crime scene tape was stretched across the front walk. A uniformed police officer stood on the porch. He glanced at me as I walked by, but I guess he took me for what I was pretending to be, just another curious kid in the neighborhood. I walked right past my place, trying to imagine what it looked like inside, what it had looked like when Billy had been found, glad that Billy had left the door open, thinking about what Detective Jones had said, that he'd probably done it for me. He'd probably done it all for me. Billy never was too bright. He should have known that no matter what, I'd rather have him with me. I'd rather not be alone.

I was out of sight of the house when I saw a car slow. It was Lew and Dan. Lew was driving. He pulled over next to me, and Dan got out of the car.

"Hey, Mike," he said. I don't think I'd ever seen him look so pale. His face was almost gray, like maybe he hadn't slept. He put an arm around my shoulder and squeezed tight. I felt like hugging him, but I didn't. I knew he liked me well enough, but I didn't think he'd want that kind of scene. "We heard about Billy," he said. "Jeez, what made him do it?"

I blinked.

"What would make a guy do something like that?" he said.

"He didn't say anything to you?"

Dan looked practically numb as he shook his head. "I haven't even seen him since the day before yesterday," he said. "We were supposed to take a run up to Barrie yesterday, to see a guy about a car. Then he called me and said he couldn't make it. That's the last time I talked to him." His eyes were kind of watery. He and Billy went way back. It made me feel good to know that I wasn't the only person who would miss him. Who missed him already. "How about you, Mike?" he said. "How you doing?"

I shrugged. What did he think?

"You got a place to stay?" he said. "You need some money or something?" He reached into his pocket and pulled out his wallet.

I shook my head. What I wanted, money didn't buy. Then, because I couldn't stand it anymore, because I had to know, I said, "Were you in on it with him?" I ducked down to look into the car, so Lew would know I was talking to him, too.

"In on what? What are you talking about?" Dan said.

"Chopping up cars. What Billy was doing."

Dan glanced at Lew, then let out a huge sigh.

"How did you know about that? Billy tell you?"

"Yeah."

"Well, that's old news," Dan said. "It's what Billy *used* to be doing. That was before." He said it like I was supposed to know before what. And I guess I did, too. "He smartened up when he had to, right? He looked after you okay when he had to, didn't he?" If you ignored the absence of groceries and how he left neatness and cleanliness up to me, then, yeah, he looked after me just fine, and I said so. Dan glanced at Lew again and shook his head. "Okay, yeah, so he did this thing."

"What thing?"

Dan peered at me. "He didn't tell you?" he said. "'Cause if he didn't tell you—"

"You mean about the car that killed Mom," I said.

Dan shook his head again. He looked like he was in pain, and squeezed the bridge of his nose between his thumb and forefinger. "You know Billy. Always thinking short-term. Always trying to make a few bucks. But he didn't know, Mike. And by the time he found out, what was he supposed to do? Get himself into trouble for something that couldn't be fixed?"

"My mom died, Dan."

"Yeah, I know. And Billy was sick about it. But the way he had it figured, he had to look after you, and he wouldn't be able to do that from a jail cell, would he? Besides, he didn't know who dropped the car. The way he told it—and I believe him—he never knew stuff like that. It was just some supposed-to-be-slick insurance scam. Some guy wants to trade in his car for a newer model. No big deal. He's paid his insurance premiums all these years and never even had a speeding ticket. He figures maybe the big rich insurance company owes him a little something in return. So he knows a guy who knows a guy who arranges to pinch his car, he doesn't even know who does the job. He doesn't know what happens to the car after that. And Billy, he doesn't know whose car it was or who took it or where everything ended up afterwards. It's supposed to be that no one gets hurt. Everyone does it, Mike." He shrugged. "It's just that, in this case, there was an angle to it Billy didn't figure until it was too late. I mean, how was he supposed to know that the guy was unloading a car that had been involved in a hit-and-run? It was one big screwup, Mike. One mother of a twist of fate. If you ask me, Billy should have just gone to the cops and told them what happened. Anything would have been better than putting a noose around his neck, right?"

For the first time that I could remember, I found myself agreeing with Dan.

He put his arm over my shoulder again. "Billy was like a brother to me, too, Mike. I loved the guy. But you know how he was. He did the best he could, but he wasn't the smartest or bravest guy around, you know what I mean?"

Yeah, I knew.

"Come on," Dan said, "what do you say we all go get a bite to eat? We should probably talk about arrangements, too, right? You're gonna have to do something."

Something about a funeral, he meant. I felt my knees buckle. I had never dealt with a funeral before. Billy had taken care of everything the last time. I let Dan steer me to the car. I got into the backseat. Lew glanced at me in the rearview mirror, his eyes dull, not playful like they usually were. As he hit the gas, a little plastic Marilyn Monroe figurine danced at the end of a chain that hung from the mirror. If Billy were here, he would have reached out and flicked a finger at her, sending her spinning—he always did. But Billy wasn't here. That was the whole point.

CHAPTER FOURTEEN

Dan and Lew took me out for burgers, and we talked about what we should do for Billy's funeral.

"We should have a party," Lew said. "A real blowout."

Dan kicked Lew under the table and shot him an annoyed look. "He means a wake," he explained.

"He's right," I said. If there was one thing Billy loved, it was a party. And if there was one thing he hated, it was funerals.

Dan chewed on a French fry and studied me for a moment. His voice was low, almost soft, when he said, "I don't know how to say this, Mike, so I'll just come right out with it, okay? I mean, there's no one else to ask. You're it. Okay?" I nodded, but inside, I dreaded whatever was coming next. "You want to bury Billy, or you want to cremate him?" he said.

I put down the burger that I had been lifting to my mouth.

"I'm sorry," Dan said. "But there are some things, they're just impossible to pussyfoot around, you know?"

Things like funerals. It wasn't his fault. And I didn't have an answer.

"What do you think?" I asked.

Dan shrugged. "These things, like most things, all come down to dollars and cents. You want to bury someone, you have to get a place to bury them and that costs big bucks. You want to cremate them, you get a little urn. It's simpler and cheaper. I don't know how much money Billy had put away and I don't know if he had any insurance, but—"

We kicked it around, Dan asking questions, Lew coming up with ideas for the wake, and me thinking how glad I was that they were there and were willing to make decisions. It was going to be cremation for Billy and a beer party for his friends, and Dan said, "If you want to, you can forget the age of majority, Mikey. Billy probably would have wanted it that way, okay?"

I wasn't so sure. Sometimes Billy called me the white sheep of the family to tease me. Sometimes, though, I didn't think he was kidding. Sometimes I thought he was hoping.

I was glad when the funeral talk was finished and we went back to Dan and Lew's place. It was the complete opposite of Riel's house. Their apartment was cluttered, none of the furniture matched, the wood floors were scuffed, and there was more stuff on the kitchen counters than in the kitchen cupboards. But it was relatively clean, and they made me feel welcome.

"I'm gonna grab a beer," Lew said almost as soon as we got inside. To my surprise, he disappeared out the door at the back of the kitchen.

"Uh, didn't he overshoot the fridge?" I said.

Dan laughed. "The beer fridge is downstairs," he said. "That's where we do most of our work." He showed me around the place. "Lew's room is all yours," he said, "if you want to catch some Zs. You look wiped, man."

"I don't want to take Lew's bed—"

Dan grinned. "Lew won't mind. Half the time he falls asleep in front of the TV. Isn't that right, Lew?"

Lew was back with his beer. "Go ahead, Mikey," he said. "No problem. Just don't touch Marilyn, okay?"

"Marilyn?" I glanced at Dan.

Dan rolled his eyes. "Five hundred bucks," he said. "He actually spent five hundred hard-earned bucks on a—" He seemed to be searching for the right words. "A china figurine."

"An original Marilyn," Lew said. "Come on, Mikey."

He led me down the hall and threw open a door. The first thing that struck me was how cluttered the room was. The second was . . . Marilyn: Marilyn Monroe posters. Marilyn Monroe calendars. Marilyn Monroe pinups. Black-and-white production stills from Marilyn Monroe movies. And, on a shelf over Lew's messy dresser, a china figurine of Marilyn Monroe, pushing down her dress as it flies up around her—like that famous picture. It was from some old movie.

"It's a real collector's item," Lew said. "It's worth about ten times what I paid for it." He lifted it gently and showed me the bottom. "She signed it herself. I bought it off a woman who hated it—said it was her old man's most prized possession. When she left him, she took it with her." He sat it back on the little shelf and straightened it so that it faced just so.

I don't know if it was grief—jeez, Billy was gone, he was really gone—or lack of sleep or the fact that for once my stomach was full, but after Dan and Lew left me, I flopped down on the bed and closed my eyes. When I opened them again, the window was black except for the nearly round silver ball that hung in one corner. The moon.

For a moment I just lay there half-awake, thinking how right it felt to be in my old room, surrounded by my stuff, in my own house—and not thinking all that hard about it because it's just there, like wallpaper, this is where I am and this is where I belong. Then the next minute, alarm, alarm, alarm! It hit me. This *isn't* your room, pal. This *isn't* your house. This is an alternate reality. The new real deal. What it is from here on in.

I sat up—boom!—and fumbled with a lamp on a small table near the bed and checked my watch. It was past ten-thirty. I buried my head in my hands and tried to stop myself from crying, but I didn't manage it. Now what, I kept asking myself. Now what?

I heard soft voices somewhere beyond the door. Maybe it was Dan and Lew. Maybe it was the TV. Maybe it was a little of both. Dan didn't have much patience for TV unless it was sports—a baseball game or basketball or hockey. Lew, on the other hand, could and would watch anything from cooking shows to fifties sitcoms. His favorite show was *The Simpsons*.

I stood up and drew in a deep breath. *First, calm down. Next, stay calm. You can't go out there and face the guys with tears running down your cheeks.* Jeez, when was the last time I had cried? Cried? Make that blubbered. When was the last time I had done that?

I knew exactly when.

I wandered around the little room. It was as cluttered as the rest of the apartment. A chair in one corner was almost invisible under a jumble of Lew's discarded clothes. The dresser was covered with magazines, CDs, empty beer bottles, videotapes—everything except the stuff you'd normally expect to find on a dresser. Every surface was piled high with things. Even the CD tower beside the door had stuff on top—a can of hair mousse, of all things, and a little basket of loose change. It was weird. All Marilyn, all messy, all the time.

For the first time I thought about the Children's Aid lady. She was probably wondering what had happened to me. Maybe Riel was, too, although I didn't care so much about that.

I ran my tongue over my gritty teeth and suddenly wished I'd brought a toothbrush with me. Clean clothes wouldn't have hurt, either, but all the things that I had from the house were back in Riel's spare room.

I opened the door and went down the hall. Sure

enough, Lew was sprawled out in front of the TV.

"Where's Dan?" I asked.

"Out," Lew said. "He'll be back soon."

"You don't know if there's a spare toothbrush around here, do you?"

Lew looked at me like I was crazy.

"Mind if I check around?" I asked.

I don't think Lew was even listening. His eyes were on the TV screen. I took that as a go-ahead.

I checked the medicine cabinet in the bathroom first. Plenty of aspirin and soap, a package of dental floss, but no toothbrush. Out in the hall beside the bathroom were three drawers set into the wall and, above them, some cupboards. I checked the cupboards first. Blankets and bedsheets, pillowcases, towels and, up top, a couple of rolled-up sleeping bags. I pulled open the first drawer. Okay, getting closer. A first aid kit. Some half-empty bottles of shampoo and conditioner. A bag of disposable razors. A couple of cans of shaving cream that, from the bits of dried foam around the nozzles, had been used if not used up. A brand new package of toothpaste and a newish-looking bottle of mouthwash. Next drawer—bingo! Not one, but two brand new toothbrushes, still in their packages. It figured. Dan didn't get that dazzling lady-killer smile of his by not brushing. I grabbed one and made a mental note to replace it with a new one as soon as I could, not that I thought he was going to freak out over it or anything. I was shoving the drawer shut when I glanced at a small pile of envelopes to one side.

Envelopes from a photo developing place. I picked one up and slid out the pictures.

They were pretty recent and mostly they were of cars. But there were a few of Dan and Lew and Billy together, all smiling at the camera. They must have got someone to take them, maybe one of the girls who were always hanging around one or the other of them. Then there was a picture of Billy, all alone, standing in front of a candy-apple-red Jaguar, leaning against it like he owned it—which he didn't—looking like he thought he was pretty cool in his black jeans and black T-shirt and black boots, dark glasses hooked and hanging down from the neck of the T-shirt, hair so blond it looked like silver in the sunlight. He looked all right. If I were a girl, I might even have thought he looked cute. I kept that picture out when I put the others back. I was going to ask Dan if I could keep it or if I could get a copy made.

I grabbed another envelope, curious now to see if there were any other pictures of Billy. Since Mom died, neither Billy nor I had taken any pictures of anything. All I had were four years' worth of school IDs. The only time Billy had had his picture taken was when he renewed his driver's license. I wanted to remember him the way he was lately, not the way he was years ago.

But the pictures in the next envelope were not as recent. Billy's hair was long in the back and short in the front, a stupid Billy Ray Cyrus cut he used to have and had stuck with way too long. I remembered when he had chopped it all off. It was the day before Mom's funeral. He had gone to the barber and had come back with his hair buzzed down to within a centimeter of his head. I never asked why, and he never explained. There were pictures of Billy with Kathy, the girl he'd been going with when Mom died. There were pictures of him with Dan and Lew, and pictures of Dan with a couple of girls, one on each side, with his arms around both of them. I didn't recognize the girls, which wasn't surprising considering that I had been ten or eleven at the time and Billy wasn't living with us anymore. Besides, Mom didn't like Dan and Lew, so they never came around the house. I'd only really gotten to know them since Mom died, and I had never figured out what she didn't like about them. I mean, compared to Billy, they were almost reliable, and Dan especially was a whole lot smarter. There were pictures of Lew, also with the girls, but they looked less than thrilled to be in his clutches. Of the three of them, Lew was the least good-looking, the least well-dressed, the one who always had a little B.O. Mostly Dan or Billy had to ask the girls they knew if they could find someone for Lew. It was funny that in all of the older pictures, Dan looked deadly serious. No wild smile. No big smart-ass megawatt grin. Guess he'd lightened up in recent years.

"Hey, Mikey," said a voice behind me, so sudden that it startled me. Some of the photographs slipped from my hand. "What're you up to?"

I turned to look at Dan and held up the toothbrush I had found. Lew was standing behind him.

"All my stuff is back at Riel's place," I said. "Lew said it would be okay if I looked around for a toothbrush." I turned to Lew for confirmation.

Dan shrugged. "No problem." He stooped to get the photos I had dropped.

"You don't look too happy in those pictures, Dan," I said.

Lew reached over and plucked a couple of them from Dan's hand.

"Yeah," he said. "The no-smile years. Felt like an idiot with all that hardware on your teeth, right, Dan? Looked like one, too."

"Hardware?" I looked blankly at him.

"You know, braces," Lew said. "You should have seen his teeth before he got them fixed. Most politicians are straighter than Dan's teeth used to be. He had to get the money together first, though. His parents couldn't pay for it. So there he was, twenty-one, with a mouth full of hardware. Didn't smile for, what, two years, right?"

Dan laughed. "Yeah, well, I've been making up for it ever since."

Maybe there was a window open somewhere, but I don't think so. I think that chill came from someplace else, someplace inside.

A mouthful of hardware. A mouthful of silvery braces. Four or five years ago, when Mom was still alive and Billy was still wild . . .

I watched Dan tuck the pictures back into their envelope and slip them into the drawer, his movements casual, his face calm, even smiling a little, like it was all okay, like nothing bad had happened, nothing that involved him, anyway.

"I'm going to clean up, then I'm going to go back to bed," I said. Maybe it was just my imagination, but my voice sounded tight and high. Dan didn't seem to notice, though. Neither did Lew. "I gotta get some sleep," I said. "I don't know what's wrong with me, but I'm really tired."

"Stress," Dan said. "Stress can really do it to you, Mikey."

I ducked into the bathroom and washed up as well as I could. When I came out again, the hall was empty and I heard voices in the living room. I slipped back into the spare room and sat down on the bed in the dark. Then I waited.

It didn't take long. An hour at the most. I heard a lock turn down the hall. The front door, I thought. Then I heard footsteps in the hallway and someone—Dan—used the bathroom. Lew must have already been asleep on the couch. I waited another thirty minutes. Then another fifteen, just to make sure. The apartment was silent.

I got up, opened the door to the spare room, and crept down the hall. There was a cordless phone in the kitchen. I grabbed the handset and crept back to Lew's room with it. I'd decided to call Riel, when, stupid, stupid, stupid, I realized I didn't know his phone number. Information. Dial information.

I was about to punch 411 when the door to Lew's

bedroom opened. Dan looked at me, then at the phone in my hand.

"Hey, Mike, what're you up to?"

"Just making a phone call."

"Yeah? Who are you calling?"

"A woman from Children's Aid. I was supposed to meet her after school today. For all I know, you guys could be in a lot of trouble because they're supposed to be looking after me and they don't know where I am."

He thought about this for a moment, then said, "You're calling her at midnight? Don't you think it could wait until morning?"

I shrugged. "Better late than never, I guess."

Dan grinned and shook his head again. "Come on, Mike, you were going to call that cop, weren't you?"

I denied it.

Dan was still smiling as he took the receiver from my hand.

"You're not being straight with me, Mike," he said.

"What do you mean?"

"You're going to tell that cop what I said about Billy, aren't you?"

I relaxed a little. "No," I said. "No way, Dan."

"If you did that, all of a sudden the cops would want to know how I knew about that and what else I know. And I don't want the cops sticking their noses into my business. You understand that, right, Mike?"

"Sure," I said. "I wouldn't want to get you in any trouble, anymore than I'd want to get Billy in trouble.

That's why I should call the Children's Aid lady. They're going to be looking for me. You know they are."

Dan seemed to consider this. I relaxed a little more, feeling almost confident that it was going to be okay, that I was going to be able to leave.

"It's late," he said at last. "You get some sleep, and we'll call first thing in the morning, okay?"

I heard a shuffling sound in the hall. Lew? Sure enough, his sleepy head appeared behind Dan.

"What's up?" he said.

"The cops are probably looking for me," I said. That seemed to wake Lew up—fast.

"Relax," Dan said. "It's nothing. Mike's just worried about Children's Aid."

"I really think I should at least call and tell her where I am," I said.

Dan held tight to the phone. "How about I get you something to settle you down and help you sleep, Mike? You really need some rest. Lew, you stay here with Mike, okay? I'll be right back."

He said it all so calmly, and his smile was so friendly, like all he cared about was me and my welfare. He squeezed by Lew, who filled the doorway. I heard him pad down the hall, going in the opposite direction from the front door. Now was my chance. All I had to do was get out and keep going. But how could I get past Lew?

Marilyn.

I whirled around, grabbed Marilyn from her little shelf above the dresser, and threw her up in the air.

"Hey, Lew," I said.

But Lew was already diving into the room, scrabbling to catch her before she smashed onto the floor. I was diving the other way, for the door. I was trying to keep from tangling myself up with Lew, which is how I managed to crash into the CD tower. It toppled left. The container of mousse on it flew right. The little basket on top of it cascaded coins all over the floor. The noise brought Dan back on the double, but by then I had forgotten about running because by then I was staring open-mouthed at the coins that lay scattered all over the floor. At one coin in particular, one that glinted like the sun in the middle of all those dull copper pennies. I could almost feel it smooth and cool and heavy in my hand.

Lew lay on the floor, clutching his precious Marilyn.

"Jeez," he said. "Jeez, Mikey." He started to get up, cradling the figurine. That's when he saw what I had seen and what Dan was looking at now. Dan's eyes were hard and cold; his million-dollar smile had vanished.

"I told you to get rid of that," he said to Lew. The fact that he said it—said it right in front of me—told me just how much trouble I was in, and probably had been ever since he and Lew had picked me up that afternoon. Then I thought, that was no accident, no chance encounter. They had been looking for me.

"Come on, Mike," Dan said. He grabbed my arm. His hand bit into my flesh. When I struggled, he said, "Don't make me hurt you, Mikey."

I don't know if it was the rumble of his voice, the

dead look in his eyes, or the pain I was already feeling from his hand clamped around my arm, but I quit fighting him. Better to stay alert and look for a chance, I thought, than to have him hurt me badly now.

He dragged me down the hall, through the living room and the kitchen, to the back door that led downstairs. Lew followed closely behind. Between the two of them, I was taken down the narrow stairs and into the garage.

Dan flicked on a light, and I saw two cars. One of them had big pieces of paper attached to it. It took me a moment to figure out that it was being prepped for a custom paint job. I peered around. There was paint and paint equipment everywhere. There were also a couple of carts of tools, and more tools hanging from hooks or sitting on shelves around the place. At the far end were the big double garage doors. To one side was a smaller person-sized door. It was locked.

Padlocked.

So were the garage doors.

"Too bad you took off on the Children's Aid," Dan said. "I hear that happens to them a lot. Kids take off. Who knows where they end up? They just disappear."

I felt that chill again, only this time I knew it wasn't a draft from a window. There weren't any windows down here. There was just me and Dan and Lew.

CHAPTER FIFTEEN

One thing I've learned is that mostly you should be glad about the everyday annoying boring things that make up maybe nine-tenths of life on a good day. Got a quiz coming up in math? Best friend acting like a jerk? Chicken burgers in the school cafeteria for the twelfth day in a row? Parents giving you a hard time over your so-so grades? Lost another library book so there goes this week's allowance? Late for your after-school job again and for sure your boss is going to chew you out? Boring, boring, annoying, boring, and you'd do anything if someone would set you free, right?

And then everything shifts.

The whole landscape.

When my mother died, I had to adjust my thinking about almost everything—from what kind of place I would live in and what would appear (or not appear) on the table at mealtime, to what was expected of me and who expected it.

Now Billy was gone and I had to adjust again. Only this time I was completely alone. Now there was no one—absolutely no one—whose job it was to make sure that I was alive and breathing, forget fed and clothed and educated. All of a sudden, everything was up to me.

And now this.

There I was, standing in Dan's garage, absorbing the look in Dan's eyes and thinking, *This is it.* That moment you never imagined. And now that you're in it, you can't believe it. It doesn't even come close to feeling real. But you know it is, because you're there, you're hearing it and feeling it and it's playing out right in front of you. Oh, and you've got a part in it. You're the guy whose name will show up in the credits at the end of the movie, way down the list somewhere. The bit part in the murder mystery. The disappeared guy. The dead guy. The corpse.

"What are you talking about, Dan?" I said, hoping, praying, ready to trade everything I had that he didn't mean what I thought he meant. "I'm not going anywhere."

"Yeah, Mike," Dan said. "You are."

I glanced back over my shoulder at Lew, who was standing behind me. He had a tire iron in his hands.

"Hey, come on, Dan. I'm not going to say anything," I said.

"Yeah?" Dan said. "You're not going to say anything about what, Mike?"

He was a whole different person when he wasn't smiling. When his face was serious like that, when his eyes drilled into you like that, it wasn't hard to imagine him breaking into Mr. Jhun's place, robbing him, and beating him so hard he died. I bet there had been no smile that night. But there must have been later, the night my mother died. Mrs. Jhun had seen his shiny mouth. It sparkled like the sun, she had said, so he must have smiled at Mom. And then what?

He had robbed Mr. Jhun's place—he and Lew. The coin proved it. And Dan had also talked to Mom the night she died. There was no doubt in my mind about that. But what else had he done? And why?

"I'm not going to say anything about anything," I said. "I swear. I got problems of my own."

Man, did I ever.

"Billy told you, didn't he?" Dan said.

"Billy didn't tell me anything."

Then there it was, that megawatt smile. "It's kinda funny in a way," Dan said. "I mean, you look at it in the right light, it's even what they call ironic."

He must have been using a whole other definition of irony than the one I knew from school.

"We only knew about it because *you* told Billy."

"Me? What did I say?"

"You told him about the keys to the place."

He meant the keys to Mr. Jhun's restaurant. But what . . . ?

"I didn't know about any keys," I said. Not until Riel had told me about them. "How could I have told Billy about something I didn't know about?"

Dan shrugged. "Billy told us about it, and he said he

found out from you. You think Nancy would ever tell him something like that?"

I shook my head. "No way. I never—"

I never said, Billy, Mom has keys to Mr. Jhun's restaurant. But there was something else. Little scenes flashing in my head, like the trailer to a movie.

Scene: Mom and Billy, in the kitchen. Mom worrying aloud to Billy about all that money being around Mr. Jhun's place. Billy saying, "How much money are we talking about?"

Cut to: A day, a couple days, maybe a week or two later. Billy at our house babysitting while Mom was out at the community college, taking a course.

Billy: "Hey, Mikey, what do you think about that restaurant, you know, the Chinese one?"

Mike: "Food's good."

Billy: "What exactly does Nancy do there?"

Mike: "Mostly she talks to Mrs. Jhun. Mr. Jhun, too. And she does paperwork for him."

Billy: "Yeah? She does it right there in the restaurant?"

Mike: "No. She does it here."

Billy: "How come I've never seen her then?"

Mike: "You're not here all the time, Billy. And you know Mom, she puts everything away when she's not working on it."

That was all I said. I never said another word. I never mentioned any keys. I didn't even know about the keys. But, man, I knew Billy. He must have gone looking. Who knew what was going through his mind? Maybe he thought he'd find cash. Maybe he was looking for more information—"Just how much money are we talking about?" He must have found Mom's box. And in the box, he must have found the keys.

"The thing about Billy, though," Dan said, "he was gutless. Lift some keys and get duplicates made? No problem. Hand the keys over to me and Lew? Again, no problem. But go with us to do the job? No way. One hundred percent the opposite, in fact, but I bet he didn't tell you that, huh? Gave us the keys, then beat it over to Nancy's place so that he'd have a watertight alibi for when it went down. Nancy could vouch for him. *You* could vouch for him."

It wasn't a good sign that Dan was telling me this. It could only mean two things. One, that he thought I already knew most of it. And two . . .

"Then he tried to get what he called his fair share. 'One-third, one-third, one-third,' he said. 'I earned mine, Danny.'" Dan snorted. "Yeah, like you can earn a fair share of anything when you're home in bed, letting the other guys take all the risk."

"Hey, Dan, I would never—"

"It was supposed to be easy," Dan said. "Wait until the old guy goes to bed. Slip in, grab the cash, slip out. Simple, right? Except the old man comes downstairs and sees us and makes a grab for this baseball bat he keeps behind the cash register. Can you beat that? The guy isn't even from around here, and there he is with a baseball bat, like he grew up playing Little League. And he's swinging it at my head like there's a baseball sitting on top of my neck and he's Barry Bonds. What was I supposed to do?"

I wished he wasn't telling me this.

"And there's Billy, sitting at home. Mr. Alibi. And he wants money for that? We gave him a finder's fee, that's all, right, Lew?"

Lew. A couple of weeks ago, if you'd asked him, he would have described himself as an honorary uncle. Now he was tapping one end of a tire iron into the palm of his hand. I had to give him credit, though, he didn't look too happy about it.

"We gave him a couple hundred, and what did he do with it?" Dan said.

The Xbox and all the games. The stuff that Mom made him take back.

"Toys," Dan said. "He spent the money on toys that Nancy wouldn't let you keep. When she made him take them back, what did he do? Trashed them."

"I don't care," I said to Dan. A lie. Probably the biggest lie I had ever told. "I don't care."

Dan peered at me. No megawatt smile. No jolly uncle grin. Just a hard look.

"You don't care?" he said. "If you don't care so much, how come you got everything stirred up? How come you got that cop involved?"

It was on my tongue to say: he isn't a cop anymore. But I didn't think that would make any difference to Dan.

"What do you want me to do?" I said. "Billy's dead.

I got no one. I just don't care anymore." I looked back at Lew. Maybe he saw things differently.

"Hey, Dan," he said, his voice quiet.

But Dan kept his focus hard on me.

"You're a good kid, Mike," he said again. Every time he said it, things got worse for me. "The trouble is, I don't know you. Not really. You're just Billy's nephew, and Billy screwed up good. He talked when he shouldn't have. You want to blame someone for the situation you're in now, blame Billy." He gestured to Lew.

"He's just a kid," Lew said, still clutching the tire iron, but looking less menacing, at least compared to Dan.

"He's just a kid who can land us some serious prison time," Dan said. "What's the matter with you? You heard Billy, blubbering about the damn car. What, you think he didn't tell Mike?"

"He didn't tell me anything," I said, "except that he had seen the car."

"But you figured out the rest, didn't you, Mike?" he said. "That's how come you waited until you thought I was asleep before you made that phone call. Calling that cop, right?"

"No, Dan—"

"And that coin, right, Mike?" He shook his head. "Look, I'm sorry it worked out the way it did. But stuff happens."

"Stuff like my mom, you mean?"

When someone has done something terrible, and when they have you locked in tight and they start talking about how you're going to disappear and then they start giving you details, you know you're in terminal trouble. I figured I had nothing to lose now. And if there was one thing I had to know—*needed* to know—it was what had happened to Mom, and why.

Dan didn't answer. Instead he said to Lew, "Get some rope."

I looked Lew straight in the eyes. Lew, who idolized Marilyn Monroe and Bart Simpson. Goofy Lew. Lew with his tire iron, tap-tap-tapping in the palm of his hand.

"Sorry, Mike," was the best he could come up with.

You see it in movies—a fellow gets himself into a jam with some bad guys. The bad guys decide to deal with the situation, which is never good news for our hero. You feel for him. But you know he's going to be fine—he's smarter than the bad guys or stronger or he has an ace in the hole. Maybe he slipped a knife up his sleeve a scene or two back that the bad guys don't know about. Maybe he has the ability to dislocate his shoulder at will, which he demonstrated in the first scene, so he can slip out of the ropes or the chains or whatever they tie him up with. You just know he's going to be fine. That's the movies.

But real life runs differently. You look at these guys, the bad guys, except they're guys you've known forever, guys you've trusted—you look at them and you think, They're not kidding. And the reason they're not kidding is that they're afraid. You can hurt them. You can tear their lives apart. You tell anyone what you know and, like Dan said, they're looking at serious prison time. You know it and they know it, and the only thing they can think of to make sure that doesn't happen is to make sure you don't talk. You see them with their tire irons and their ropes and you check those padlocks one more time—there's no way out. You're done like Thanksgiving dinner, and pretty soon all that's going to be left are the bones.

"How did she know?" I said. If it was going to come down to that, then at least I had a right to know. At least I could take that with me.

"What?" For a moment, Dan looked confused.

"My mom. You killed her because she knew, right?"

"Down on the floor, Mike," he said. "Face down."

I did what he told me, and I asked my question again.

"Put your arms behind your back. Lew, hurry up with that rope."

I heard a *shwok*, and a coil of rope landed on the ground beside me.

"It was my fault," Lew said.

I craned my neck around, trying to get a look at him, but he must have been standing somewhere behind Dan because I couldn't locate him.

"It was stupid," he said. Then he stopped talking. The silence almost drove me crazy.

"Jeez, Lew, you've been at my house a million times. You carry on like you're someone special in my life. You can at least tell me what happened. You think I don't deserve that?"

Dan wrenched my arms back, and I felt the rough rope bind me tightly.

"We were out there that night," Lew said. "Just taking care of business, you know? And she stopped at a phone booth and was fumbling in her purse and then she saw us." He came closer. I saw his feet and twisted my neck to look up, way up, at his face. "She asked if I had change for a five," he said. "She was late, and she wanted to call home and tell you she was on her way."

"You don't have to," Dan said. I wasn't sure what he meant.

"I wasn't thinking, I guess. I don't know. I dug into my pocket and brought out all this change." He stopped and looked at Dan. "The old man had that coin," he said.

Mr. Jhun's lucky gold coin. The one that had been stolen the night he was murdered. The one I had just seen in Lew's room.

"Dan told me maybe a hundred times, get rid of that thing. But it was real gold, you know. You ever walked around with a real gold coin in your pocket?"

I didn't say anything.

"Nancy saw it. She pretended like she didn't, but she saw it. She said she changed her mind about making a call, she'd just go home, she was worried about you. Mike, we didn't have any choice."

We didn't have any choice.

Dan stood up and tossed him a key ring.

"Unlock the door," he said.

Lew's feet stayed where they were for a moment.

Then they walked away. Dan grabbed my hair and pulled my head back. When I opened my mouth to yell, he rammed a balled-up rag into it, almost choking me.

"Okay, Mike, on your feet," Dan said. He grabbed the rope around my wrists and pulled, yanking my arms almost out of their sockets. I staggered to my feet.

I watched Lew unlock the padlock on the garage door. I know he was working at normal speed—inserting the key into the lock, turning the key, pulling on the lock to disengage it, unhooking the lock from the metal loops in the garage door, engaging the lock again and setting it aside, tossing the keys back to Dan, who caught them easily with the hand that didn't have a firm grip on me. But it all seemed to move in slow, slow motion. Each step seemed to take minutes instead of seconds. And the whole time I was watching, I was thinking, *This can't be happening to me. These guys can't possibly be going to do what I think they're going to do. They can't possibly have done what they just told me they did.* I was on my feet only because Dan had such a firm grip on me. I couldn't feel my legs. If Dan had let go, I'd have crashed to the floor.

I don't know if I heard it first or if Dan did, but he tightened his grip on my arms and *sshhed* Lew. Then he yanked me back to the wall and shut off the lights. In the darkness, I heard thumping. It seemed to be close by. And then I realized: someone was knocking on the front door to Dan's place.

"Mike? You in there?"

CHAPTER SIXTEEN

"Mike?"

It was Riel. He wasn't more than a few feet from me, but I couldn't call out and tell him that.

"The door," Dan hissed. "Lock it."

I heard Lew fumble to find the lock in the now dark garage. Dan cursed in my ear. He yanked me toward the workbench and scrabbled around for a few moments, opening and closing drawers.

"I can't find it," Lew said, his voice sharp with panic.

I heard a click. Then a rumbling, scraping sound as the garage door started to roll upward. Silvery light from the moon and outside lights appeared first at the ground level, then crept higher and higher. Lew scrambled back toward Dan, looking around wildly for where he had left his tire iron.

I saw a pair of boots, a pair of legs, a torso, then Riel,

standing alone, framed in the double-wide opening. He peered inside.

"Mike, you okay?"

I nodded, even though there wasn't a sane person anywhere on the planet who would call my situation anywhere near okay. I was tied up. Something hard was jammed into my back. Dan's fingers bit into my arm.

"You boys want to come out of there?" Riel said, as if he were asking if Johnny could come out and play.

Lew edged closer to Dan and glanced nervously at him.

"It's Dan, right?" Riel said, still friendly, trying to keep things light, I guess. He stepped into the garage.

"Stop there," Dan said. He pulled his hand away from my back and held it up to show Riel what he was holding. A gun.

Riel stopped and raised his hands slightly so that Dan could see they were empty. But he held his ground.

"Why don't you let the kid go?" he said. "Things are bad enough already, wouldn't you say?"

Dan brought the gun down, in front of me this time, pointing it right at my chest.

"The police had a long talk with an Arthur Sullivan today," Riel said.

A tiny part of my brain wondered who Arthur Sullivan was. The rest of my brain was 100 percent focused on the gun in Dan's hand. From where I was standing, it looked as big as a cannon.

"He told them the whole story, Dan," Riel said. "He said that all he was looking for was a new car and a little relief from his insurance company. He said he didn't plan on his car being used to kill anyone."

I locked onto the answer fast and hard. Arthur Sullivan was the guy who owned the car that had killed Mom. The car that had been reported stolen. The car that Billy had chopped.

"He told them who arranged things for him," Riel said. "He described you so well, Dan, even a blind man could make an identification."

Dan glanced at Lew. "Start the car," he said.

Lew took a step toward the car.

From clear across the garage, I heard Riel sigh. "You really think that's a good idea?" he said.

Lew froze.

"Hey, you got nothing to say about this," Dan said. He sounded angry, which made me nervous. He was still pointing his gun right at me. "I've got the kid. I've got the gun. I make the decisions." He looked at Lew again. "Start the car!"

"How far do you think you're going to get?" Riel said. I couldn't figure him out. He was standing alone, framed in the garage door. If he had a gun, I didn't see it. But there he was, talking like he was holding all the cards. "I know you have the kid. The cops know you were in possession of the car that killed Nancy McGill. It's not going to be much of a stretch to tie at least one of you to the restaurant killing, either. I guess you know they found blood at the scene that didn't belong to the victim. Which one of you boys sustained injuries?"

Lew's eyes were wild now.

"Jeez," he said. "Now what are we going to do?"

"Let the kid go," Riel said.

"Who's going to make me?" Dan said. Slowly the gun moved away from me and toward Riel. "You?"

Even in the dim interior of the garage, I could see the shadow of a smile on Riel's lips.

"What? You're going to shoot me?" he said.

As he took a step forward, one of his hands swung behind his back. I felt Dan's hand tighten on me again. The gun he was holding swung all the way toward Riel. I struggled. I saw Riel's hand come back up. Then a light sliced across my face, blinding me and Dan. A gun went off, the shot almost deafening me. The beam of light vanished as the flashlight Riel had been holding crashed to the ground. Riel crumpled. I kicked Dan as hard as I could, and in that instant he released his grip on me. Then someone yelled, "Down!" and suddenly the garage was flooded with lights and filled with cops. Lew stood perfectly still, eyes wide, hands above his head. He kept saying, "Don't shoot, don't shoot." Dan was ordered to lie spread-eagled on the floor of the garage. Two cops with guns drawn stood above him while a third cop handcuffed him. Another cop—Detective Jones—helped me to my feet. He pulled the rag out of my mouth and then turned me around and worked at untying my hands.

"You okay?" he asked.

I kept trying to twist around to see how Riel was. But

when I could finally see, he wasn't there anymore. I felt like I had just been locked in a deep freeze. Everything went cold. I saw spots in front of my eyes. I swung around, scanning faces.

Then I saw him.

On his feet. Another cop was with him. Detective Jones's partner, Detective London. He was helping Riel with something. It took me a moment to figure it out. He was helping Riel take off a vest. Riel handed it to the detective and came over to me.

"You okay, Mike?"

I nodded. A great big lump in my throat was making it hard to breathe. I felt like I could burst into tears at any moment.

"I thought—"

"It's okay, Mike," he said and threw an arm over my shoulders. "It's all okay."

» » »

It turned out that Billy had done one good thing—he had told me about the car. That little piece of information had led the police to question the owner of the one car they couldn't account for, the one that had been reported stolen. At first, Riel said, Arthur Sullivan played the good citizen. His car was stolen, he reported it, he was a straight-shooter. Then the detectives told him about the hit-and-run and how they knew it was his car that had been involved. They told him how much trouble he could be in because his car had been used in a homicide. That's when he had crumbled and told them everything he knew, which was just enough to identify Dan.

"Yeah, but how did you know where I was?" I asked Riel. We were at a police station. Riel was drinking coffee. I was drinking hot chocolate.

"One of the uniformed guys saw you walk by the house this afternoon. He saw you get into a car. Your friend Vin filled us in on Billy's friends and gave us Dan's name. I took a chance. I couldn't figure out where else you might be."

I was at the police station for a long time, telling the detectives what had happened and what Dan and Lew had told me. Riel sat with me the whole time. When I had finished telling them everything I knew, Detective Jones looked at Riel. It didn't take a genius to figure out that there was something else, something they hadn't told me yet.

"What?" I said.

"It's about your uncle," Detective Jones said. He looked at Riel again. Riel turned to me.

"Billy didn't kill himself," he said.

"I know."

Riel frowned.

Dan had said, "What would make a guy do something like that?" It had taken a long time for it to register. I guess I hadn't wanted to believe it. Dan and Lew were Billy's friends. They'd been buddies for almost as long as I could remember.

"Dan knew . . . how Billy died," I said. "I didn't tell him, and it wasn't in the papers. What I don't get is why."

"They figured if Billy had told you, he might decide to tell the police, too. I'm sorry, Mike."

I wished I could go home. I wished I had a home to go to.

CHAPTER SEVENTEEN

With his best friends sitting in jail, waiting to go to trial for murder, Billy's funeral turned out to be a lot smaller than I had planned. Some of the guys he worked with showed up. So did Carla and a couple of his ex-girlfriends, including Kathy, who had stayed with me the night Mom had died. She cried more than anyone else there. Vin showed up with his parents, both of whom came up to me afterwards and told me I would always be welcome at their house. Always. Sal and his dad came, too. His dad shook my hand but didn't say anything. Jen showed up, which surprised me. She hung back until everyone else had gone, then she approached me. Her eyes were red.

"I'm so sorry," she said. She kissed me on the cheek and sort of hung there for a moment, like there was something else she was going to say. But I guess there wasn't, because finally she just turned and walked away.

Mr. Scorza came. I saw him sitting near the back of the room, and I kept hoping he would leave right afterwards so that I wouldn't have to talk to him. I still felt ashamed about what had happened. But he didn't leave. Instead, he walked straight up to me and shook my hand and told me how sorry he had been to hear about Billy. I told him thank you. He didn't offer to give me back my job. I hadn't expected him to, but, really, I had been hoping.

» » »

One month to the day after Billy's funeral, I went down to Children's Aid and sat in a windowless office and talked to Margaret Phillips for more than an hour. Mostly she kept asking me if I was sure.

"I'm sure," I said.

"It can be a difficult adjustment," she said.

As if I didn't know that. But what was the alternative? "I'm sure," I said again.

"It will be just on a trial basis at first," she said. "And you'll have a caseworker checking on everything. If there are any problems, or if you change your mind, we can always talk about it. It doesn't have to be forever, you know."

I told her I knew.

Riel was waiting for me when I came out of the office.

"What did she say?" he asked.

"She kept asking me if I was sure."

He smiled. "They asked me the same thing," he said.

"They kept telling me how hard it is to be a foster parent."

"And?"

"I said I was sure. I told them any kid who was soft on old ladies would probably work out just fine."

"Huh?"

"That's when I knew you were okay, Mike. When I talked to Mrs. Jhun's neighbors. When I found out how you visited her and helped her." He smiled. "You're still going to have to go to court on that other thing, though."

"I know." But I wasn't dreading that nearly as much as I had been. "What about you?"

He looked surprised. "What about me?"

"You going to stay teaching school?" I kept thinking about him saying, *We* looked into it.

He smiled and shook his head. "We're only six weeks into the school year," he said. Then, with a sigh, "I guess I haven't decided yet."

I went home to a house that wasn't my own, a house that looked like no one had really lived in it, even though Riel had been there for a couple of years. While I set myself up in the back bedroom, Riel got busy in the kitchen. Then he went upstairs to change. When the doorbell rang, he called from upstairs for me to answer it. Dr. Susan Thomas was at the door. She had a bottle of wine in one hand and some cut flowers in the other.

"Hello, Mike," she said.

When Riel came downstairs, he looked less scruffy. He also smelled of aftershave. He took the wine, asked me to find something to put the flowers in, and showed Dr. Thomas into the kitchen.

Supper was good. After I had cleared the table, when the two of them were still sitting there, sipping wine and smiling at each other, I said, “Okay if I go over to Vin’s?”

Riel thought about it a moment.

“Okay,” he said. “But home by midnight, okay?”

Home by midnight.

“Okay,” I said.